JORGE IBARGÜENGOITIA was born in 1928 in Guanajuato, a small mining town in the center of Mexico. When he was a child his family took him to Mexico City where he lived until recently. From 1953 to 1960 he wrote ten plays, some of which received a modest success. In 1961 he wrote a play based on the 1929 assassination of a Mexican president by a militant Catholic. The play received an international award from the *Casa de las Américas*, but was officially condemned by the Mexican authorities.

In 1963 the author wrote his first novel, a satire on the Mexican Revolution that has been published in nine countries and seven languages. Since then he has written a book of short stories, two successful plays, and five novels, one of which won the National Prize for a Novel in Mexico. THE DEAD GIRLS is his first book published in English.

Ibargüengoitia has also taught Spanish literature at American universities. For eight years he wrote a by-line in *Excelsior*. He now lives in Paris with his wife.

THE DEAD GIRLS

JORGE IBARGÜENGOITIA

Translated from the Spanish by
ASA ZATZ

 A BARD BOOK/PUBLISHED BY AVON BOOKS

THE DEAD GIRLS (*LAS MUERTAS*) is an original publication of Avon Books. This work has never before appeared in book form.

AVON BOOKS
A division of
The Hearst Corporation
959 Eighth Avenue
New York, New York 10019

First Bard Printing, January, 1983

BARD TRADEMARK REG. U. S. PAT. OFF. AND IN
OTHER COUNTRIES, MARCA REGISTRADA, HECHO EN
U. S. A.

Printed in the U. S. A.

OP   10   9   8   7   6   5   4   3   2   1

Some of the events described herein are real. All the characters are imaginary.
J.I.

Contents

I
Double Revenge

1

One can picture them: all four wearing dark glasses, Ladder, driving, hunched over the wheel, Brave Nicolás, beside him, reading *Strength* magazine, in the backseat, the woman, gazing out of the window, and Captain Bedoya, asleep, his head bobbing.

The cobalt-blue car strains its way up Dog Hill. The January morning is sunny, the sky immaculate. Smoke from the houses floats on the plain. The trip is long, the road straight as far as the top of the grade, after which it descends, snaking through the Güemes Mountains between the cactuses.

Ladder stops in the town of San Andrés. Finding the three asleep, he wakes the woman to pay for the gasoline and goes into the lunchroom. He breakfasts on pork cracklings in green tomato sauce, refried beans, and an egg. When he is on his second cup of coffee with hot milk, the three come in, groggy. He observes them with compassion: it is for him the beginning of a day, for them the end of a carouse. They take seats. The captain, proceeding with caution, asks the waitress, confidentially, "What would be nice and tasty that you could recommend?"

Ladder gets up, goes to the street, and takes turns around the square with long, slow strides, hands in pockets, toothpick between his teeth. Despite the bright sun, an icy breeze is blowing that forces him to button his jacket. He pauses to watch a group of shoeshine boys pitching coins against a wall in a variation of the game unfamiliar to him. Continuing his stroll, he reflects on whether the Mezcala people could be any stupider than those of Plan de Abajo. He stops briefly again to read the inscription on a monument to the Boy Heroes: "Glory to those who died for their country . . ." when he sees his passengers emerging from the lunchroom, the captain and the Brave Man in civilian clothes combined with parts of their uniforms, the former wearing his cavalry boots and the latter an olive-green field jacket; the woman, Serafina, in a rumpled black dress which, as she steps into the car, bares a dark thigh and shows her armpit. Having settled back, they blow the horn peremptorily, summoning the driver to come and get them on their way.

The road takes them by historic spots: through Aquisgrán el Alto, at the entrance to which there is a sign that says: "Mr. President, they stole our water!" and where Serafina orders a halt to quench her thirst with a bottle of orange soda; through Jarapato where Ladder stops to drop a peso into the collection box of a church being built with contributions from drivers; through Ajiles where they buy cheeses; past Cazaguate Hill where the captain asks to be let out to pass water— "to sign the roll," as he puts it; and, to San Juan del Camino, which has a Miraculous Virgin, where they take a break.

Serafina goes into the church (subsequently, it was learned that she lit a candle, knelt before the Virgin to pray for good luck in the undertaking, pinned a votive offering of a little silver heart on the red velvet hanging, and gave thanks in advance as though her wish were already granted). The three men, meanwhile, seated at a table in the ice cream parlor, order frozen custard, discuss what they are about to do, and reach the decision that it had best be done in the light of day. When Serafina joins them, she disagrees and orders the operation to be carried out at night.

This means at least three hours to be killed, which they spend sleeping under a sapodilla tree just outside Jalcingo.

The sun is setting when the dogs of Tuxpana Falls begin barking at them. It is a wide, dark town with dusty streets, a naked electric bulb on a pole every two hundred meters. Tuxpana Falls is noted for its guava orchards. Every house in town is said to have one, but all their doors are shut. The children play in the streets.

Ladder stops the car on a corner where a group of people are seated under a kerosene lamp eating *pozole*. Brave Nicolás gets out, approaches them, and, addressing the cook, says, "Pardon my rudeness, but where might I find a bakery?"

She informs him that Tuxpana Falls has three bakeries and gives him directions. They drive from one end of town to the other and from bakery to bakery without finding what they are looking for until the last.

"This must be it," says the Brave Man, who has gotten out of the car three times and bought three bags of crullers.

All climb out. The men go around to the trunk of the car as Serafina walks over to the bakery. The building is humble, its two doors are the only ones open on the street. Approaching cautiously, doing her best to avoid being observed, Serafina peers into the shop and sees a man seated behind the counter and a woman doing accounts. She returns to the car. Very deliberately, Ladder, a length of plastic hose in his hand, siphons gasoline out of the tank of the car into a can. The captain and the Brave Man remove two automatic rifles from the trunk, insert the magazines, snap the bolts to test them, making considerable noise. The captain hands Serafina a pistol.

What takes place after that is uncertain. The Brave Man stands in one doorway and Serafina in the other. She addresses the man behind the counter, "Don't you remember me anymore, Simón Corona? Maybe this will remind you!" And, aiming high, she shoots. The man and woman are under the counter before the gun is empty. The Brave Man lets go a burst into the bakery then says to the captain, standing beside him, "You fire now, my captain."

"No, I am covering." His weapon is trained on the opposite sidewalk in case of an attack from the rear.

11

The Brave Man carries out the final phase of the action. He enters the bakery, splashes gasoline on the floor, steps outside, lights a match, and throws it on the wet boards. The gasoline catches fire with a dull clap and flames leap through the doors. A couple of women have come to buy bread and stand outside the shop gaping in fascination. Serafina, returning to the car, hustles them on their way, snapping at them, "What do you want? This is none of your business! Go home!"

Everybody back in the car, Ladder turns it around, making a more than usually elaborate maneuver, and drives uncertainly through the streets until finally, recognizing the road leading out of town, he speeds up, leaving Tuxpana Falls as they entered, to a chorus of barking dogs.

2

The fire damage to the bakery was estimated at thirty-five hundred pesos. Forty-eight regulation-caliber shells were found on the floor by the police. All the bullets were lodged in the walls. One grazed the skin of the shoulder and right arm of the clerk, señorita Eurdemia Aldaco, who had been in the rear of the bakery. She and the baker, Simón Corona, the only persons on the premises at the time of the incident, suffered minor burns.

The official on duty at the local office of the Department of Justice arrived at the first aid station, where the victims were being attended, at 8:30 P.M., and asked the doctor if they were in a condition to be interrogated, to which he answered that the woman had been given a sedative but that the man was conscious. The agent found Simón Corona in a room lying on a cot, bandaged, and put questions to him.

Q: Describe the incident as it happened.

A: He was sitting behind the counter waiting for señorita Aldaco to finish adding up the day's sales when he heard a voice saying to him, "Don't you remember me anymore, Simón Corona . . ." and so forth.

Q: If he suspected anybody who might be responsible for the assault?

12

A: He did not *suspect* anybody. He knew exactly who the person responsible was because he saw her right in front of him with a pistol in her hand, and that it was señora Serafina Baladro who lives at . . . an address in the city of Pedrones, state of Plan de Abajo, appears here on the record.

Q: What could have been the motive behind the said party's action?

A: He was embarrassed to admit it, but he had lived with señora Baladro on several occasions in the past— "We would be together for a time and then we would separate for a time because she was difficult to get along with"—until he left her for good during a trip they made to Acapulco because he realized then that she did not deserve his love. She was so resentful over his leaving her that she hunted for him for over three years until she finally located him.

Q: If he knew the other parties who took part in the assault?

A: He did not, but could give a description of one of them since he saw him up close while he was selling him half a dozen crullers a few moments before the incident — "He was not short but not tall and he was not young or old."

Q: If he had any idea how the attackers had obtained a regulation automatic rifle and .45 caliber pistol?

A: He did not, but that during the times they lived together he noticed that she had connections with the army.

The deposition having been taken and the record prepared and signed, the official went through the regular procedures prescribed by law, which consisted of notifying his superiors, naming suspects, and requesting the attorney general of the state of Mezcala to request the attorney general of the state of Plan de Abajo to request the representative of the Department of Justice of Pedrones to order the chief of police of that city to arrest señora Serafina Baladro for questioning.

Two weeks passed and the inhabitants of Tuxpana Falls were beginning to forget the incident when the official received the following wire:

"Recall declarant for questioning and determine if a clandestine burial was carried out by him in 1960 together with the accused, Serafina Baladro."

At his second session with the Department of Justice representative, Simón Corona wished to have several points clarified before making any statement: Whether it was compulsory or optional for him to give the information? ("Did you come here of your own free will or were you ordered to come?" "Of my own free will." "Then, it is optional.") Whether Serafina Baladro had been arrested? ("It says here 'the accused,' which means she is already in jail or going to be.") "Whether it would lengthen her sentence if he answered "yes" to the question? ("Probably.")

Satisfied with the replies, Simón Corona told the official the story of Ernestina, Helda, or Elena. The verbatim record was read back to him, the declarant found it accurate and signed at the bottom. That signature cost him six years in prison.

II
The Case of Ernestina, Helda, or Elena

1

Following is the case of Ernestine, Helda, or Elena as told by Simón Corona while in prison:

I saw her through the trees in the square walking in my direction but didn't want to believe it. That woman in black carrying the patent leather purse couldn't be Serafina. She looked like her and was dressed like her but it couldn't be her. Whether it was or not, I felt my knees begin to tremble. Could it be possible that I am still in love with her? I asked myself.

I was leaning against a pole next to the ice cream stand in the square waiting for it to be twelve o'clock, the hour I had to see somebody in the Treasury office about a tax matter. The woman kept coming through the trees and the closer she got the more she looked like Serafina. No, it can't be her, I said to myself again just to calm my nerves. She is living in another town. There is no reason for her to come to Pajares. She was getting closer and closer, thinking, she told me later, that the man by the ice cream stand couldn't be me. When I was finally able to make out those high cheekbones, the slanty black eyes, and that hair pulled back tight, it was too late. It was Serafina, all right, and she had me cornered.

She came straight over to where I was, opened her mouth as if she was going to smile—I just caught a glimpse of that broken tooth of hers—and slapped me in the face.

I didn't move. She turned and walked away. I looked around to see if anybody had witnessed my shame. The only one there was the ice cream man who turned the other way and got very busy scraping out a can. If he had laughed I would have broken his jaw, but he didn't and all I could do was go off in the opposite direction from the way Serafina went.

It was the same as happened to me other times. She would do something nasty to me and I was the one who ended up feeling guilty about it. I put that slap out of my mind like other things she did two years before, like her getting mixed up with that traveling salesman, and the sock under the bed. All I had on my mind was one thing: I could not live without Serafina. I had left her, but I didn't care about anything in this world except her taking me back.

I walked through the crooked streets of that town with the sun beating down, the flies pestering me—it being June—and saying to myself, She still loves you. That slap in the face proves it.

I regretted that I didn't get down on my knees the minute I recognized her and beg her to forgive me for leaving her. I would have liked to have said to her, Take me back! Instead, I just stood there without opening my mouth and when she walked away I didn't follow her. I was sure that this time I had lost her forever—and I couldn't bear it.

That was what was going through my mind as I came to a corner. I turned my head to look up the street before crossing and there she was again, a long block away, walking slowly like a person with nothing to do, killing time. Serafina must have been around thirty-eight then, but seeing her like that at a distance she looked like a young girl to me. She stopped in front of a shop window for a while, crossed the street, bumped into a man carrying a big bundle and, just as I was making up my mind that it would be better for me to go my way before she saw me, she saw me.

Once again, I did nothing but stand there until she

16

came up to me. "What are you doing in Pajares?" she asked.

I told her the truth—that I had to see about a tax matter.

"That's what I am here for, too," she told me.

It seemed as though our meeting on that strange street in a strange town at such an hour of the day was the most natural thing in the world; as if we hadn't separated two years before after a tremendous quarrel; as if we hadn't come together again just twenty minutes before with a slap in my face. Our relationship was always like that. I never knew what to expect from her.

I looked at my watch. It was after twelve. I was about to suggest that we go together to see the man about the taxes when she said, "Take me to a hotel."

Her lips were painted a strange color, a sort of violet.

We stayed in the Commerce Hotel until after eight o'clock that night. When we checked out we were hungry, so we went to a restaurant on the square. Serafina said she was in a hurry to get back to Pedrones, and the woman I was living with at the time must have been worried waiting for me in Tuxpana Falls, but when we finished eating, instead of saying goodbye and each of us going our own way to take care of our own responsibilities, we went back to the hotel and stayed until the following day.

If I had gone home the next morning, that meeting with Serafina would have been just another of the many things that have happened to me in my life that I can hardly remember anymore and would have no reason to be telling about. But I didn't go home. When I opened my eyes I thought of the woman I was living with and realized how upset she must be, probably imagining I was lying by the side of the road somewhere covered with blood. This made me feel even less like seeing her. I put on my shirt, went to the window and looked out at the laurel trees in the square and the birds singing. Then I glanced over at the bed, at Serafina asleep, and felt like waking her up.

I waited for her to shower and dress, and when she was sitting in front of the mirror fixing her braid, I could see that her reflection looked different from her face, something I had noticed before. A strong feeling

17

rose up inside of me as I recalled happier times and I said to her, "I'll drive you to Pedrones."

But she was not going to Pedrones. Whatever her hurry had been, it didn't matter anymore. She was going to San Pedro de las Corrientes to have dinner with her sister Arcángela. Since I didn't want to leave her, I said, "I'll drive you to San Pedro, then."

I owned a 1955 Ford at the time, which I had put in a garage there in Pajares to be repaired. If, when I called for it the mechanic had said to me, as I fully expected, "It's not ready, come back in the afternoon," I would have walked Serafina to the bus depot, we would have said goodbye then and there, and my life would have been entirely different. But the car was ready, it started up as soon as I put my foot on the gas pedal—and here I am with a six-year sentence ahead of me.

To get from Pajares to San Pedro de las Corrientes you take a steep grade where no matter how good your eyesight is you can't see anything but rocks all around. But when you reach the top you come to a view that is something else again. To the left you can make out the whole Guardalobos Valley, one of the most fertile spots in the whole state of Plan de Abajo. Not a piece of ground goes uncultivated in this valley—where there isn't alfalfa growing, there's strawberries, and what isn't a cornfield is a wheat field. Even the huisaches that grow along the sides of the road are green and beautiful. I always did like that valley, but felt even more so about it that particular morning because I was so happy to have Serafina sitting next to me, relaxed, her hand resting on my leg. I felt as though I didn't have a care in the world and I said to her, "Don't you feel your heart swell when you see that?"

But, while I was looking in one direction she was looking in the other—toward the Güemes Mountains—which was why she misunderstood and thought I meant that what made my heart swell was the statue of Christ that stood on the peak looking west, as though, the people say, he was trying to embrace the whole state of Mezcala. She took her hand off my leg and said, "You never stop bellyaching about going back to that lousy hometown of yours, do you?"

That's how it always was with Serafina; I would try to

18

say something nice and she would come back with something mean. I didn't let it bother me this time, though, because I knew very well what it was she held against me. Each of the times I left her I went back to Tuxpana Falls, which is in the heart of Mezcala. That is why she always had it in for the town. You couldn't even mention the name of the place in front of her, or even say that it had good guavas. That morning it was as though I had said "Tuxpana Falls" to her because she got moody and said to me, "You think I am not good enough for you because I run a whorehouse."

That annoyed me and I answered her, "I never left you on account of the whorehouse and I wasn't looking at that statue. I was looking in the opposite direction. Besides, what is the point of throwing things up to me that can't be helped, when you know that all you are going to accomplish is to spoil such a pretty day?"

I guess I must have gotten through to her. She put her hand back on my leg and didn't say anything more.

I should have thrown her out of the car when she made that nasty remark. Both of us would have been a lot better off.

We bought avocados in Huamantla and sat down under an acacia tree to eat them. It was very quiet; the only sound was of turtledoves cooing. From where we were you could see the dark soil around the dam and teams of oxen plowing. With all that calm around us we forgot our quarrels—and even that we had both come to Pajares to take care of some business and hadn't accomplished anything. Serafina said, "If only life could be like this all the time!" or something of the kind.

Before going back to the car, we went into the ruins of an old textile mill out of curiosity, and there under the caved-in roof in that empty building she wanted me to have her once more, and I did. We continued our trip after that and arrived at San Pedro de las Corrientes at two o'clock in the afternoon.

Serafina invited me to have dinner with her sister but, frankly, I did not feel like having to face Arcángela. I knew that her opinion of me had never been very high and I imagined that after I left her sister in 1958 it must have reached a new low. And so, I decided that the adventure would end at the door of the México Lindo.

19

"I'll say goodbye and God bless you here in the car," I said to Serafina.

But fate had written a different story. As I turned the corner of the street where the cabaret was, the first thing I saw was doña Arcángela standing on the sidewalk. It looked as though she was in mourning. In spite of the heat, she wore a shawl over her head and there was a girl on either side of her. The three of them were looking in my direction as though they had been waiting for me.

I had no choice now but to do just exactly what I didn't want to: Stop the car, turn off the motor, get out, and greet her. When she saw me opening the door, she gave me a look out of those little pig's eyes of hers as if to say, "this is all we needed!" But it passed quickly, and she stretched out her arms and said affectionately, "Simón! How nice to see you!"

After that she hugged me and even gave me a kiss. That was just when I should have gotten suspicious, but I didn't, even though I noticed that this demonstration of affection took her sister as much by surprise as it did me. I explained to her that I was only passing through, but it did no good—it was just dinnertime, there was a hot meal all fixed, and she was so glad to see me again. She insisted on my driving the car into the patio through the gate next to the cabaret. "That way you won't have to worry about boys doing any mischief to it."

As I was driving in she began to discuss some matter with Serafina that seemed to be very serious. When I got out of the car, I noticed something unusual for that time of the day—most of the girls were standing around in the outside corridor leaning over the wall talking to one another or looking down at me.

While we were walking into the dining room, doña Arcángela took me by the arm and said, "I am glad to see you back. The men my sister has had since you left have been a disaster."

I wanted to explain that I was not "back," but only passing through, but she never gave me a chance. She sat me down at the table, put out a bottle of very special —according to her—tequila, told the girls with her to bring me the limes and salt, and then left the room with Serafina.

The Baladro sisters went out one door and the girls out the other, leaving me alone in the dining room for nearly an hour sitting at the table with that bottle in front of me. I took a swig from it every now and then as nobody ever brought me a glass. When the door finally opened and Arcángela and Serafina came in, I got up and said to them, "I'm leaving. If I am going to have to sit here by myself and go hungry, I might just as well be riding in my car."

"Simón," Serafina said to me then, "my sister has a very serious problem."

She explained that one of the girls who worked in the México Lindo had died the night before and they didn't know what to do with the body.

"Hold a wake and then take her to the cemetery," was my advice.

Arcángela then pointed out that the deceased had died in an act of violence and could not be buried in a regular cemetery without informing the authorities.

"And I can't permit that," she finally said, "because it would cause trouble for me."

There was no other way out but to take the body and dump it where nobody would see. But then came the second part of the problem: Ladder, the only taxi driver the Baladros trusted, couldn't be located.

"That's why I am so upset," said Arcángela, drying the tears she seemed to be shedding.

And so I answered, "Don't worry, Arcángela, I'll take the body in my car and drop it wherever you tell me to."

As soon as the words were out, I regretted I ever opened my mouth, but it was too late. The truth of the matter is that it had been too late all along. For things to have turned out differently, it would have been necessary for me not to have gone to Pajares the day before about the tax matter. Not five minutes earlier I was just a hungry man sitting and waiting to be served some food and now here I was obligated to take a dead body over to the mountain.

They were very grateful when I made the offer. Serafina rested her hand on my leg. I was sure that she would have given herself to me right then, but I was in no mood. Arcángela dabbed at her tears and left the dining room. A moment later I heard her in the patio shouting, "Tell Ladder never mind."

Later, I found out that it wasn't that they couldn't find Ladder, but that he wanted a thousand pesos for the job.

After a while, Arcángela came back with some folded bills, which she handed me, saying, "Toward the gasoline."

It was five hundred pesos, which I put in my pocket. At least I had enough spirit to set a condition. "I'll take the deceased wherever you say," I told them, "but I'm not touching her."

When they finally brought the soup in, I wasn't hungry anymore.

2

He states that his name is Simón Corona González, he is forty-two years of age, married, Mexican, residing in Tuxpana Falls; that he is a baker by trade, cannot read or write, but signs his name; that he is a Catholic, is not a habitual drinker of alcoholic beverages, and does not smoke marijuana or use other drugs or narcotics. Questioned as to whether he was making this statement voluntarily, he answered affirmatively.

He states that he met Serafina Baladro in 1952 in Pedrones in a house she was running on Molino Street; that the same day he met her he became her lover and that they lived together for two years, after which he left her to return to Tuxpana Falls; that in 1957, at the request of the same Serafina Baladro, he went back to her and they lived together again for one year, after which he left her a second time and returned to Tuxpana Falls again.

He also states the following: In the year 1960, I ran into Serafina by accident in the city of Pajares and she wanted me to drive her to her sister Arcángela's house in San Pedro de las Corrientes. When we arrived there, Arcángela said to me, "Drive your car into the patio," and I did. They brought me into the dining room and gave me a bottle of tequila to drink. Later on, both sisters came in and said to me, "As soon as it gets dark, go along the highway and dump the body of a girl who died

22

into the gully." So, we drove on the Mezcala highway in my car until we came to a curve where Arcángela said, "Stop here," and I did. I did not watch while they were putting the deceased into the car, but I had to help get her out. She had gotten stiff and they weren't able to pull her out of the trunk between Arcángela, Serafina, and a girl by the name of Elvira who came along with us. While we were carrying the body toward the edge of the gully, the sack that was covering it fell off and I got a good look at her face: She had sharp features and her eyes were very big and wide open. According to what I heard, her name was Ernestina, Helda, or Elena. When we returned to San Pedro de las Corrientes, as Arcángela was getting out of the car in front of her house, she said to me, "If I ever find out that you have spilled what happened tonight to anybody, I'll look for you and I'll find you no matter where you are hiding." Afterward, Serafina and I went to Pedrones. We stayed together there for another six months and then I left her for the third time and returned to Tuxpana Falls.

III
An Old Love

1

Juana Cornejo, known as the Skeleton, related the following with respect to the relations between Simón Corona and Serafina Baladro:

Of all the señores she had, don Simón was the most polite. He always called me "señora Juana" and he would call the girls "señorita." He never asked for anything without saying "if it isn't too much trouble," and whenever he left the room it was always "with your permission."

He was always up early and would come into the kitchen when I was still busy lighting the fire.

"Good morning, señora Juana."

Sometimes he would leave and be gone for a long time, but when he came back to the house, the first thing I would hear the following day was don Simón saying good morning to me.

He would tell me about Tuxpana Falls while I was fixing breakfast. For him it was a great thing to go walking along the banks of Stony River there of an afternoon, holding hands with a girl.

They say that don Simón spent his mornings sitting on a bench in the square listening to music and his afternoons playing dominoes in a bar. He came back to the house every night, but never went into the cabaret. He would go straight to the señora's room and we never saw him again until the next day.

24

Sometimes, he would be very thoughtful and sit looking at his plate of *chilaquiles* instead of eating them and then he would say to me, "I live with one foot in the stirrup all the time."

He would leave his breakfast half finished, and instead of walking to the square, he would go out to the yard and sit under the guava tree. After a while the señora would go out and ask him what was wrong. He must have been telling her that he was tired of the life he was leading in Pedrones and that he wanted to go back to Tuxpana Falls and she must have told him, all right, to go ahead and go. Then, she would come into the kitchen for breakfast, holding back her tears.

These were not like the quarrels they had on account of jealousy, but just difficulties that came up every now and then when don Simón got the urge to leave. He went away three times for a long while and came back twice, but he wanted to leave a lot of other times and couldn't.

One day he got his things together and went through the house saying goodbye to everybody. "I'm leaving on the five-thirty bus," he said to us.

That was before don Simón owned a car.

He was in the middle of his goodbyes when there came a knock on the door. I opened and it was Captain Laguna with another soldier. They asked for don Simón.

I knew they were no friends of his, so I told them, "Oh, he left quite a while ago."

It must have been Divine Providence that kept those men from entering the house, because if they had they would have found don Simón around the first turn in the hall. They did not go in, but they didn't believe me, either, because they stood on the corner waiting for him. When I told don Simón that the *federales* had come looking for him and were waiting outside, he didn't dare step out on the street for months, let alone go back to Tuxpana Falls.

That time he was lucky, but other times it was not so good for him. The soldiers caught him once in San Pedro de las Corrientes and again in Muerdago. They brought him back to Pedrones and locked him up in the guardhouse, where they gave him a very bad time making him clean up the filth. It went on that way until señora Serafina got him out through Colonel Zárate, who

25

was a friend of hers. Don Simón came back looking as though he had seen the devil, ate a great pile of tortillas, and didn't say a word for a long time about living with one foot in the stirrup.

I asked him one day what it was he had on his conscience that the soldiers should be so hot on his trail. He explained to me that he was a deserter, that he had joined the cavalry as a young fellow, but couldn't take the hard life. So, he lived one step ahead of the law for twenty years, because he quit three months before his time was up.

2

Regarding her relations with Simón Corona, Serafina Baladro said:

When Simón came to the house on Molino Street for the first time, he was not very civilized. I saw him standing by himself at the bar, not talking to anybody. And that big fellow, I thought to myself, I wonder what's on his mind. To get him over his shyness, I pulled him out on the dance floor, but he couldn't dance a step. I am a very good dancer, though, so I showed him and he picked it up little by little.

"How about buying me a drink?" I said to him after a while.

The yokel had to admit that all he had on him was fifteen pesos.

"You can thank the Lord," I told him, "that the owner took a liking to you."

He never realized that it was me that the house belonged to. It was the same story as with other men—I looked so young and pretty that they couldn't imagine I was the madam.

"Hand over the fifteen pesos," I said to him, "and the rest is on me."

To be honest, I must confess that I really went for him. We sat down at one of the tables and he told me he came from Tuxpana Falls and was a baker.

"You must have crumbs in your belly button," I said

to him. "I want you to be sure and wash thoroughly before you get into bed with me."

I took him to my bathroom, which was like nothing he had ever seen before. As I watched him standing there, naked, twisting the faucets, I felt the blood rush down to the pit of my stomach. Simón was a big dumb brute, but very sweet.

I trained him. If he is anything at all today, he owes it to me. When I first knew him, it was like he'd just come down out of the hills.

Our life together had its ups and downs from the start. We were happy most of the time, but every once in a while I could feel that my business was coming between us. For instance, it would make him jealous if I looked after the customers, talking to them or sitting down at the tables with them. It bothered him that I went to bed at two or three in the morning. "That's my work," I would tell him. "If I don't do it, what in the hell do you think we are going to live on?"

And he didn't like the idea that I was supporting him.

"If you don't want to be supported, then work," I would say to him. "Doing nothing is not compulsory."

I suggested that he take charge of the beer and soda bottles or of giving out the tokens to the girls. He could at least have checked up on the cabaret every once in a while to see if a customer didn't need a drink, or whatever.

"I'm not a pimp," he would answer. "I'm a baker."

The truth is, during the years he lived with me he didn't have to lift a finger to earn a peso.

Of the three periods Simón and I were together, the last one was the best. He reproached me less and I was really crazy about him. I felt so happy that I began to have a yearning to see the ocean.

"Take me to Acapulco," I said to him.

He had the car fixed up, I took fifteen hundred pesos out of the cash box, and off we went.

I should have figured, from the time we got on the road, that something bad was in store for me. It was very hot. I was wearing black and didn't know which of my clothes to take off next. I was anxious to get my first sight of the ocean, and was expecting to see it every

27

time we went around a hill, but all there would ever be was another hill. And wasn't it just my luck that the moment I dropped off for a few minutes was right when the sea came into view and when I woke up there we were in the town! We stopped at a little hotel that had a sapodilla tree in the front patio. The room cost thirty pesos. I hardly closed the door before I had my clothes off and flopped on the bed. A minute later Simón was climbing on top of me.

"Leave me alone," I said to him, "can't you see I'm dying of the heat?"

Simón got up without saying a word, combed his hair, put on a clean shirt, and went out.

I regretted what I said the minute the words were out of my mouth. I began wondering if he might not leave me for another woman in this strange place; I had always heard that Acapulco was filled with temptations. A long while passed before I dared go out and look for him. I was afraid I was never going to see him again.

But that's not what happened. I found him three blocks away sitting on a bench just like when he listened to the music in the square in Pedrones. I was so happy to find him that I cried in his arms. After some supper we went dancing at La Quebrada.

The first thing we did the next morning was to buy swimming suits and go to the beach. I didn't dare go into the water, but just sat under one of those thatched umbrellas with a glass of beer in front of me watching Simón get tossed around by the waves. While I was there a boy sold me tickets for a cruise around the bay on a boat with a band. We had something to eat and then went to the docks to look for the boat, which we finally found. There was a bar aboard and we drank and danced. When the sun began to set we stood there watching as it sank into the sea. At that moment, I felt as though this was the happiest day of my whole life and I said to Simón, "Do you love me?"

He told me he did and so I proposed selling the business and getting out of prostitution, giving him enough money to open a bakery, and going to live in Tuxpana Falls together, which was where he liked best to be.

It made him very happy when I said that.

28

After we got off the boat, we went walking through the streets holding hands like newlyweds. As soon as we were back in the hotel room I took off my dress and said to Simón, "Now I do want you on top of me."

When he was on top of me I felt like I never had with anybody else and that the love between Simón and me was forever. That is why I told him the story of my life.

I told him everything, even that I had fixed it with Colonel Zárate to send soldiers after him to lock him up in the guardhouse and give him a hard time whenever he left me.

I was hardly through saying this before I could see his face get serious. So, I explained to him: "I did what I am telling you because I love you so much."

He didn't answer, but just got out of bed and, with his back to me, began dressing.

"You're angry at me, aren't you?" I asked.

"Let's go and have something to eat," he answered without looking at me.

I put on my clothes in a hurry, saying to myself, Now you put your foot in it!

We went out and walked along in silence. All at once, Simón stopped and said to me, "I'm going over to that store across the street to buy a bottle of rum. Now, pay attention to what I tell you. You wait for me right here on this spot where you are standing and don't move because if you do, I might not find you when I get back from the store."

I wanted to please him, so I told him I would wait wherever he said. I saw him cross the street and go into the store. I waited there just as he told me to. Quite a while passed and I began to get worried. Could he have dropped dead in there while he was buying the bottle? I didn't dare cross the street to go to the store to see. What if he gets here the minute I've gone and doesn't find me? That will make him even angrier. But, when I saw that they were beginning to pull down the metal shutters of the shops, I couldn't stand it any longer and went over to the store. Simón was not there, but I noticed that there was another door to the side street. It was then I realized that the love I had thought eternal only a little while before was already over.

29

When I got back to the hotel, they told me that Simón had "left in the car." He didn't even have the decency to pay the bill.

That is what I got for being honest with a man who didn't deserve it.

IV
Enter Bedoya

1

In describing her general health and state of mind during the months following her separation from Simón Corona in Acapulco, Serafina Baladro mentions headaches, a morbid predilection for sitting alone in the darkened dining room eating canned sardines and bread, not wanting to talk to anybody, a total lack of interest in the business, and a feeling of disgust for men. She was continent for the first time in her life, for forty-seven days, she neglected her appearance—she did not fix her braid for nearly a month—and she says that just the thought of a man putting his paws on her turned her stomach. Toward the end of this period, she had an emotional—but platonic—involvement with one of her girls by the name of Altagracia, whom she subsequently fired.

She suffered from insomnia. The final hours of the night and the early hours of the morning were spent with her eyes wide open, in imaginary conversations with Simón Corona during which she reproached him for his ingratitude, proved to him how everything she had done was for his good, and drew up lists for him of the favors he owed her. Lying there in the darkness, she says that she did not dare take her arm out from under the sheets for fear that she would feel a cold hand on it.

On the last of these sleepless nights she realized that Simón was not going to come back to her and she made up her mind that if he was not to be hers, neither would he be anybody else's. That is to say, she decided that she was going to comb the earth until she found and killed him. She imagined herself, pistol in hand, shooting, and Simón Corona in a corner with holes in his shirt, his face twisted in pain. After dwelling on this image for a time, she fell into a deep sleep.

She made her first trip to Tuxpana Falls, the town she loathed, the following week. In her patent leather purse she carried a .25 caliber pistol, in which she had no confidence, and a pair of scissors in case it failed.

She walked around the town, which looked horrible to her, asking for Simón Corona, but could not locate him. However, she did meet up with two women who had lived with him. Simón had left one of them to go with Serafina, left Serafina to go with the other, and the other to go back to Serafina.

Those three women, who had hated one another for two years, two of them knowing each other by sight and the three only by vague references to one another, met in a restaurant and hit it off famously, joined by the common bond of one man's perfidy.

"I bear him such a grudge," Serafina said, "that I can't rest until I find him so I can do something to him that will really hurt."

Since the other women offered no objections nor indicated any reservations with respect to infamy, the three made a pact in accordance with which the two who lived in Tuxpana Falls agreed to notify Serafina by wire the moment Simón Corona showed up in town. Serafina, on her part, agreed to pay five hundred pesos to either for reliable information as to his whereabouts. The understanding having been reached, they toasted liberally in a Mexican brandy. It was the first time three drunken women had ever been seen alone in a Tuxpana Falls restaurant.

The pact was fated never to be consummated. After leaving Serafina in Acapulco, Simón Corona worked in a bakery in Mezcala for three months. When he finally returned to Tuxpana Falls, his two former mistresses kept their end of the bargain, each sending a telegram to Serafina in Pedrones. However, around that time Serafina completely lost interest in the search. Neither of the women received the five hundred pesos from her and two years and nine months went by before she took the revenge related earlier.

2

The first time she saw Captain Bedoya, Serafina Baladro was standing on the corner of Soledad and Cinco de Mayo streets in Pedrones. He was riding a dapple-gray horse—borrowed—wore a helmet, and carried an unsheathed saber in his hand. The band was playing "The Dragoons' March." It was on the occasion of the Sixteenth of September parade of the year 1960. She says she noticed him because his horse was different from the others and because he was darker than any of the other soldiers—an entire regiment—who passed. He did not notice her. After the parade was over, Serafina went home and did not see or think of the captain again until five months later when she met and recognized him.

During this lapse of time, Captain Bedoya may be pictured riding another mount—a chestnut horse, government property—which is picking its way along a rugged path in the Güemes Mountains. The day is hot, insects buzz around the captain's head, and the morning glories are in bloom. A contingent of soldiers rides behind him in a file, pushing aside the branches with their hands. Ahead of him goes a man on foot, a peasant wearing sandals and a broad-brimmed hat. He is an informer.

The path grows steeper and narrower, and when it appears to be coming to an end, the peasant stops and raises his arm, indicating something on the other side of the ravine: "The flowers [poppies] are over there."

The ambush may be imagined: Two other peasants come to the ravine—which appears to be deserted—carrying sacks in which to pack the crop; their terror when they realize they are surrounded by the *federales*; the torture, something simple like a broken finger or roasted foot. They are not heroic and tell the name of the person who provides the seeds and buys their production.

33

Background material is lacking on what followed. It is not known how Captain Bedoya learned that Humberto Paredes, the person accused, was Arcángela Baladro's son, nor what intuition led him to visit her instead of notifying the police to make the arrest.

The detachment, having accomplished this brilliant action—it was the first plantation it had succeeded in uncovering—returned to the base and the captain wrote up his report, in which he mentioned taking the prisoners and burning the crop, but not that he had obtained the name of the person responsible. When he finished, he removed his uniform, put on civilian clothes, and took the Scarlet Arrow bus to San Pedro de las Corrientes.

The interview with Arcángela put his mettle to the test. At first, she treated him arrogantly, thinking he was selling something; then she took him for a health department inspector looking for a bribe—the México Lindo toilets were never in proper working order. When he explained that the matter he wished to discuss concerned Humberto Paredes, she ushered him into the dining room, figuring it was a friend of her son who had come to borrow money. The confusion was annoying; the explanation distressing.

With a firmness that surprised him more each time he recalled the incident, the captain insisted on imparting his message from start to finish: that the señora's son was a drug dealer; not only was he a lawbreaker, but he had been denounced and was practically in custody. Following this declaration, the captain was obliged to observe—in a matter of minutes that seemed like hours —the painful transition in a mother from ignorance to realization of the truth.

During the first moments of incredulity, Arcángela insulted the captain. "You are lying," she screamed at him. He remained impassive. He repeated the accusation. Arcángela then sought to explain to the captain all that she, a mother, had undergone: that she wanted her boy to be a doctor, and had even made the sacrifice of parting with him so that the youngster would not be exposed to unfavorable influences and could become a person of consequence; that she had spent a fortune on his schooling, and now she was forced to face the stern reality—her son was a drug dealer.

34

"How would you expect me to feel, Captain? All the work and privations of a lifetime thrown to the wind on account of a boy's recklessness."

She wept copiously. Picking up the white tablecloth stained with coffee, she used it to dry her tears. In the silence that reigned as Arcángela did this, Captain Bedoya had time to say, "Now, I don't want to get the boy into trouble . . ."

The captain left the México Lindo with five thousand pesos in his pocket.

This was Captain Bedoya's first contact with the Baladro sisters. Several months later, when Serafina, in her thirst for revenge, wanted to buy a more powerful weapon than the pistol she owned and to hire a teacher of marksmanship, Arcángela recommended Captain Bedoya as a trustworthy person.

3

Serafina wanted a large-size pistol, even if it meant having to hold it with her two hands to fire it, even if the kick would almost wrench it out of her grip, even if its report was ear-splitting, and even if the bullet, on entering through the victim's chest, would tear a great hole in his back. All these drawbacks were offset, in Serafina's opinion, by the assurance such a weapon gave that after justice had been meted out the "executed" culprit would not come stumbling toward her, his eyes staring like a crazy man's, arms outstretched as though he meant to embrace her.

Having made the recommendation, Arcángela then arranged a meeting. Captain Bedoya arrived at Serafina's house on the evening agreed upon at eight o'clock sharp, went to the barroom, and asked to see the proprietress.

Serafina, who was then in her period of continence, had decided that she would be polite but aloof in her treatment of the captain. Her plan was to meet with him in one of the private rooms, explain what she required, find out if it was feasible, and how much it would cost. If the price was acceptable, they would come to an agreement and the deal would be considered closed. She thought that at this point she would send for a few of the girls and order some bottles to be brought in, while she herself, as she rose from the table, would invite the captain to be her guest, make himself at home, drink his fill, and indulge his every whim. At this juncture she would say good night, leave the private room, and go about her business.

However, something happened at the outset of the interview that Serafina had not anticipated. When the captain walked into the private room, she recognized him as the darkest man in the regiment—Captain Bedoya is almost black.

"Don't you ride a dapple-gray horse?"

The captain sensed the implicit compliment. He felt impelled to tell the truth: "That is a horse I borrow, señora."

"Señorita, please!"

Captain Bedoya begged pardon, made the correction, sat down, accepted the brandy Serafina offered, and was proper and accommodating. "What was it the señorita wished?" "A large pistol." She explained the features she was interested in. He recommended a regulation .45 special. He could get one for her for twelve hundred pesos and deliver it in two weeks' time with a supply of one hundred cartridges.

"Do you want some money in advance?"

"Not one centavo."

She also needed somebody to teach her to handle the weapon. The captain promised to take her to a deserted spot where she could practice until she had acquired thorough mastery of the piece. How much would he charge for the classes?

"Not one centavo."

The deal was closed. The moment had now arrived when Serafina was to get up and call in the girls. She says that she has no idea what made her linger there chatting with that very homely man. She served him another drink and questioned him about army life, remarking that it was said to be one of considerable austerity. The captain spoke eloquently of forays on horseback, of going hungry and suffering thirst, of long nights on guard duty under the pouring rain. Then, all at once, conversation came to a sudden halt.

36

Serafina noticed that the captain had put his right arm under the table and, then, she felt a hand on her abdomen. She says that she became alarmed but did not know what to do.

Serafina terminated her continence that night and forgot all about revenge.

4

Serafina met Captain Bedoya on February 3, 1961. His influence upon the destinies of the Baladro sisters over the months following that date was decisive. He had promised the pistol in two weeks, but was lucky and obtained one in three days. He packed it in a shoe box together with a supply of one hundred cartridges and, carrying it under his arm, appeared for the second time at the house on Molino Street, went into the barroom and asked to talk to the proprietress. Serafina emerged, radiant, to greet him, escorted him to her room, where he handed over the pistol and she the money, and—the bargain having been concluded—they spent the night together.

Three days later, the captain put in his third appearance at the house on Molino Street. This time it is eleven o'clock in the morning and he is in uniform. He knocks at the door of the house because the cabaret is closed, and when the Skeleton opens it, he asks for the señorita—Serafina was "señora" to everybody else, but "señorita" to him. After making him wait in the hall for a while, she appears—breathless and blushing—in a lavender bathrobe. He says that he has come to give her her first lesson with the pistol.

Serafina dressed rapidly and put on a wide-brimmed hat with a ruffle to protect her from the sun. She thought he was going to take her to a deserted spot in the country, as he had said, but such was not the case. They took a Scarlet Arrow bus to Concepción, the village where the captain was stationed.

(This trip of Serafina's—to a village she had seen before only from afar as a cluster of houses in the middle of a plain—was fateful in her life and in the lives of the other protagonists of this story. Concepción is not on the Mezcala highway that links Pedrones and San Pedro de las Corrientes, but is connected to it by a three-kilometer-long side road.)

The captain had concocted cross-country marches and field exercises so that nobody would be in the camp at midday except the squad on guard duty. Serafina received preliminary instructions from the captain on the handling of firearms in general. Following this, she fired her first clip—erratically—on the detachment's small firing range with no indiscreet onlookers or accompaniment of mocking remarks. When the session was over, the captain took her to the commanding officer's quarters, but the cot was too narrow and the floor too cold, making it necessary to move the typewriter and make love on the desk under a contour map of the military zone, after which he invited her for dinner at the Gómez Hotel.

She says that it was during this meal—the regular six-course dinner—that she realized that she had fallen in love with Captain Bedoya. She noted that it was only with effort that she could recall Simón Corona, that she was no longer obsessed with revenge, and regretted having spent twelve hundred pesos on a pistol that left her ears ringing after every shot.

She must have said to the captain, "Tell me the story of your life."

Whereupon, he must have told her about his wife in Mexico City, whom he met, conquered, seduced, and impregnated at the graduation dance of the Military College; about their four children—especially, the little girl, Carmelita; about the day his wife caught him eating tamales with another woman in the city of Puebla; of the scene she made and how he slapped her until she fell to the floor. He must have also told her that the couple got together every two or three years in a vain attempt to patch up their marriage. (Note: Those reunions came to an end because the captain was fated to live with Serafina for three years, happy ones for both, until they had to separate to begin serving their sentences—he in the men's penitentiary, she in the women's prison.) To conclude, the captain must have complained about being lonely. Serafina must have felt sorry for him.

The captain called for the check, paid it, and left a one-peso tip—he never gave more or less and was hated by all waiters. They then went to the arcade. Serafina stood among the shoeshine boys contemplating the square. It was at this moment that it dawned on her that Concepción would be the ideal town in which to open a third whorehouse.

V

The History of
the Houses

1

Señora Eulalia Baladro de Pinto states:

The newspapers wrote that my sisters inherited the business from my father, that my father was notorious in Guatáparo for his dissolute life, and that he was shot by the *federales*. A pack of lies! My father was a respectable man, a storekeeper, a person who never set foot in a house of ill fame, and who did not live in Guatáparo but in San Mateo el Grande, where we—his three daughters—were born, and where people remember him to this day with respect and admiration. He never had trouble with anybody, least of all the *federales*. He died in the year 1947 in San Mateo from a pain, having confessed and received communion and, fortunately, without ever knowing that my sisters were involved in a way of life he would have disapproved of.

My sister Arcángela became the proprietress of a house of vice by accident. She was a moneylender; one of her clients could not pay up and she had to take over some of his properties, which included a small bar in Pedrones on Gómez Farías Street. She tried out managers for months, but they were all dishonest so she had no choice but to run the place herself. She made such a success of it that in a couple of years she was able to open the house on Molino Street in Pedrones, which became famous.

Years after that, thanks to a politician friend of hers in the state of Mezcala, she got a license to operate a business in San Pedro de las Corrientes. She came to see me at that time and said, "I am moving to San Pedro. Would you be interested in taking charge of a little business for me that I have on Molino Street?"

I was married to Teófilo and had all I needed, but I was curious to know what sort of business it was in case I might be able to run it without neglecting my responsibilities at home. That was the first I knew of what my sister was doing. I could hardly believe my ears.

"Better dead," I told her, "than running one of those places."

Arcángela took offense at this answer and we were not on good terms for years. When I turned her down, she made the offer to my sister Serafina. Whatever her faults, Arcángela was always in favor of keeping business in the family. Serafina accepted because she was young, inexperienced, had just gone through a disappointment in love, and was working in the Aurora textile factory as a spinner. She took over the Molino Street place and Arcángela went to live in San Pedro de las Corrientes where she opened the México Lindo, which was to become the most popular cabaret in the city.

For years it seemed like God was with them. While my husband and I lost everything three times through honest work, my sisters were getting rich off immorality.

2

Arcángela Baladro states:

The prostitution business is simple. All you have to do to be successful at it is to keep strict discipline.

The girls come down from the rooms at eight o'clock in the evening and file by me so I can check on them to make sure they are clean, neatly dressed, and have

41

combed their hair. The man behind the bar sets his cash register on zeros. The jukebox is plugged in and the metal shutters raised. The customers begin to arrive. Some are already familiar with the place and go straight over to the girls they prefer while others feel strange or are shy and would rather stand at the bar and have a drink or two until they make up their minds. When I notice that time has gone by and they are still at the bar, I send over one of the girls who is not busy to attend to them. Most men will go along with the first one who invites them to a table.

In my houses it is forbidden for the girls to drink at the bar. Sometimes, a customer will prefer to wait for a particular girl who is working upstairs to be free. As long as he pays for what he drinks, a customer is welcome to stand at the bar for as long as he pleases. Sometimes, a group of men will come in who want to sit down at a table by themselves without female company, which is all right, too. They can do anything they like, as long as they pay. There is one thing I will not permit, though—which is usually done by students—and that is for anybody to pick out a girl, dance piece after piece with her, and then leave without having spent a peso. To prevent this kind of behavior, the jukebox is rigged up so that there is an intermission between numbers for a rest and a drink. Everybody has to go back to the tables when a number is over. It is forbidden for anybody standing at the bar or the entrance to go out on the dance floor, for the girls to charge for dancing, or for them to sit down at a table without ordering. After each round, the waiter hands the customer a check for the amount consumed and gives the girl a token. The customer is required to pay his bill before leaving, in a nice way, and in cash.

All drinks served in my houses are legitimate. In twenty years nobody has ever been able to say he was not served exactly what he ordered. Even the girls are served what they ask for. If somebody wants rum, a bottle of rum is uncorked, and what goes into his glass is what was originally inside that bottle.

The cabaret has two doors, one to the street and one to the house. Anybody can come inside and whoever has paid up can go out through the street door. When a cus-

tomer at a table with a girl feels like spending some
time alone with her, he can ask her to take him to her
room. She will say yes because it is forbidden for her to
say no. The customer pays his check, the two of them
leave the table and go out of the cabaret through the
door to the house. This door opens into a hall where the
stairs are. The room attendant's table is at the foot of
these stairs. She is the one who tells the customer the
price because not all the girls cost the same. The customer pays the attendant and she gives the girl a token
and the man a towel. The customer and the girl go upstairs to her room where they may stay as long as he
has paid for. When they are through, they must come
down together. This is important so that the room attendant can be sure that the customer has not mistreated the girl. The customer may, if he wishes, go
back to the cabaret or he can leave the house by the
street door. The girl must return to the cabaret and con-
tinue working. A good worker earns three, four, and up
to ten tokens a night.

3

Testimony of the employee Herminia X:

I was born in the village of Encarnación, state of Mezcala. We were very poor. I was the third of eight children. I had a job as a nursemaid when I was fourteen. I
earned twenty-four pesos a month.

A woman by the name of Soledad came to my house
one afternoon and spoke to my mother. She said she
could get me a job as a servant in Pedrones where they
would give me my food, a room, and two hundred pesos
a month. My mother wanted me to go that same night
with señora Soledad.

There were two other girls in the bus who were also
going to work as servants. When we got to Pedrones, we
slept in señora Soledad's house. I knew as soon as I went
into that house that this family was not like other families, because there were women standing around in the
hall in their slips. Señora Serafina accepted me but not

43

the other two girls who left with señora Soledad and I never saw them again. Señora Serafina took me upstairs to a room and said, "This will be your room. You can keep your things here and have nothing to worry about."

As soon as she said this she went off and left me in the room by myself. I sat there for a long time and didn't dare to go out. In the afternoon, señora Serafina opened the door. I got frightened because there was a man with a mustache with her.

"This señor is a very good friend of the house," señora Serafina said to me. "His name is don Nazario. He wants to see if you've been broken in yet."

(A detailed description follows of her first experience, which is harrowing. She says that she suffered terribly in the beginning, but that she became used to it and even got to enjoy the life. She says she earned a lot of red and blue tokens and owned as many as fourteen dresses at one time. She complains that no matter how much she made it was never enough to pay off what Serafina deducted for room, board, the clothes she bought, and the two hundred pesos Serafina was sending to her mother each month—the declarant and her mother were never in touch by mail because the former did not know how to write or the latter how to read. She also complains that the two hundred pesos never reached her mother. She found this out eight years later when she met her by chance in a market. She says that she never wanted to see her family for fear that they would be ashamed of her because of what she had become.)

Testimony of Juana Cornejo, known as the Skeleton:

I met the señoras Baladro by accident. I lived on a farm and needed money because my little girl took sick. I went to Pedrones to look for work and walked from house to house knocking on doors until I came to the one where señora Arcángela opened. She said to me, "Sure, there is work in this house but not for a servant. If you are willing to be a whore, I have a job for you."

I accepted and she advanced me twenty pesos for medicines which did no good because my baby died a few days later. I stayed on with the señoras.

44

(A list of the places she worked follows. She tells how
señora Serafina appointed her room attendant and reports the instructions she received from her: "Nobody
leaves without paying. If a customer makes a row, call
Ticho [the bouncer]." She says that she never had any
problems with her bosses in the twelve years she held
that job. She finishes by stating: "The señoras never
had any complaints about me and I have none about
them because they let me have what I needed, which is
why I say they were straight women and if the police
put us in jail it was just hard luck.")

4

For years the Baladro sisters had the idea of opening a
third place of business. They were aware that since both
the Molino Street and México Lindo houses were located
within zones of tolerance—that is, red-light districts—
a certain type of apprehensive customer would not pa-
tronize those establishments as frequently as they, or
the madams, might like for fear of being recognized in
the early hours in such a neighborhood. Serafina felt
that for this reason Concepción was the perfect town in
which to establish the new enterprise: It is well situ-
ated, being twenty kilometers from Pedrones and
twenty-three from San Pedro de las Corrientes, and so
small and little-frequented that its existence is practically a secret from the world.
Serafina Baladro relates the beginnings of the Casino
del Danzón as follows:·

Hardly a week after I saw Concepción for the first
time, Hermenegildo—Captain Bedoya—brought me the
news that he had found a lot that was made to order for
putting up a building for the business. Twenty-two meters frontage by eighty-eight meters deep. It was owned
by two elderly ladies who had to raise the money to put
their brother into an institution for the insane operated
in Pedrones by the Sisters of the Divine Word. The asking price was thirty-three thousand pesos.
I liked the property the moment I saw it, but my sis-

45

ter put up objections without ever having laid eyes on it, simply because she had taken it into her head that anything Hermenegildo recommended had to be bad.

"I introduced him to you to sell you a pistol," she said to me, "not to be your lover."

And I answered, "I suppose I have a right to live my own life, or don't I?"

Well, one afternoon, Hermenegildo and I were waiting for her in front of the lot to show it to her, knowing beforehand that she wasn't going to like it. She arrived in Ladder's car in a cloud of dust. Even before she was out of the car she was finding fault with the place: It was full of holes, the walls were made of adobe, and things like that. While we were waiting to be let in, she said that its number, 85, was bad luck because the figures added up to 13.

But, as soon as she was inside, her attitude changed. She approved of the size of the lot, the walls, the two trees—one an avocado and the other a lemon tree—the bougainvillea vines, and the price.

"This," she said when we came to the rear of the lot, "is where I am going to put up a chicken coop."

Before taking the final decision, the Baladros consulted a *licenciado* by the name of Canales—a lawyer who held an important post in the state government—regarding possible problems that might arise in obtaining a license to operate a new business. He assured them that there would be none. This was at the time Governor Cabañas had just taken office, long before anyone could have dreamed he might one day crack down on prostitution.

Serafina and Arcángela decided to buy. They put up the money in equal parts and the property appears in the deed in both their names. It should be noted that Captain Bedoya received a commission from the sellers for getting them a customer who was willing to pay such a stiff price, and he collected another commission from the buyers for finding them such a reasonable property; he was given five hundred pesos of the fee paid to the notary and kept the fifteen hundred pesos for himself that the sisters gave him to distribute among important persons of the township.

This was accomplished by the middle of February and

46

on the twenty-eighth, the Baladros commissioned an architect to draw up plans for "a whorehouse the like of which had never been seen in these parts." This architect, in Pedrones temporarily, came from Tijuana where he was reputed to have built a number of brothels. Nobody knew that he was on the run from a dissatisfied client. The Baladros gave him an advance of five hundred pesos.

They were delighted with the plan: fifteen rooms and fifteen baths; a cabaret decorated to represent the ocean bottom—when one looked up one saw sharks and devilfish hanging from the ceiling; two private salons, one done in Arab style, the other in Chinese; and an indoor swimming pool, the purpose of which was not clear to anybody since none of the girls and only an occasional customer knew how to swim.

The five-hundred-peso advance to the architect was all he ever received from the Baladros for the plans, because on the night he delivered them he learned that his whereabouts had been discovered and fled, but his pursuers caught up with him as he stood at the urinal in the men's toilet in a lunchroom in Tehuacan and put eleven bullets into him.

The Baladros constructed the building from the plans under their own supervision, with the technical advice of a contractor, the suggestions of a young man who had decorated a beauty parlor in Pedrones, and the surveillance of Captain Bedoya "who was like one of the family," visiting the construction site daily—it being close to the army post—and checking on it as though it were his own property.

5

The outcome of this effort was named the Casino del Danzón. Seeing the building at the present time (1976) it is hard to believe that it was built only fifteen years ago. It looks like a ruin of some ancient civilization— the young decorator had designed a stucco bas-relief for the facade that has crumbled to pieces. Remnants of the sign are still visible on the marquee which reads:

An old man opens the door. He is the caretaker, a retired policeman, who, for twenty pesos—or less—permits the curiosity seeker—or a group of them—to enter the place where the iniquities occurred. The caretaker accompanies the tour with an explanation.

Here is the cabaret. It is lighted by a single bulb. In the center of the dance floor there is a hole three meters in diameter with heaps of dirt around it. The tables and chairs are piled up in a corner; two plaster devilfish have fallen to the floor and are smashed to pieces; a shark hanging from the ceiling by its tail, sways—drafts blow through the room—his jaws two meters from the floor. An illuminated aquarium that occupies almost one entire wall is nearly destroyed, its lights all out. The seaweed and cardboard jellyfish that used to dangle like garlands are gone, as are the globes whose light, according to a description, "between green and violet in color, is diffused from bluish glass spheres that resemble giant soap bubbles . . ."

There is a balcony in the upper part of the wall opposite the aquarium—an unexpected location—its railing gone.

The elements have caused considerable deterioration in the Baghdad Salon. The window frame has been carried off and there is a hole in the ceiling. The caretaker reports that the walls are covered with moss during the rainy season and that swallows build their nests there in the spring. This room, which has a black and yellow floor, is where the "show" used to take place that made the Casino del Danzón famous. People came all the way from Mezcala to see it. Later, in the grim period, the Baghdad Salon was one of the "sealed rooms."

The swimming pool has been empty practically since the opening night—the water was too cold and nobody was brave enough to go in. The caretaker's family uses it to store utensils and junk.

All the rooms open on a corridor and remind one more of a convent than a whorehouse. Their furnishings have remained, since the Casino's legal status is still unsettled. The women lived in spaces barely ten meters square, and were scarcely able to move around the huge beds. In addition to the bed, each room has a wardrobe, a dressing table with a mirror, and a chair with a rush seat. Every cubicle has its own tiny bathroom.

Each woman had some possession in her room that distinguished it from the others: a Divine Countenance hanging on the door, a painted glass pitcher, a clay head of a Red Indian, a photograph of a friend, an electric iron, and so forth.

After exhibiting the rooms, the caretaker leads the visitor to the yard in the rear to see the excavations—the main attraction. It seems that the tour generally ends here. However, if the tip is generous, he will conduct the visitor to Arcángela's room and show him, by way of a bonus, a photograph of a corpse pinned to the wall. It is of the Baladros' mother whose picture was snapped as she lay in her coffin with four tapers around it.

When the visitor is back on the street after the tour, he should note an important circumstance: There are only two two-story buildings on Independence Street, the Casino del Danzón and the house next door, the owner of which was señora Aurora Benavides who spent six years in prison because of this particular feature of her home.

VI
Two Incidents
and One Snag

1

The Casino del Danzón was inaugurated by the Baladros on the night of September 15, 1961. Among those who attended the celebration were: *licenciado* Canales, the private secretary of the governor of the state of Plan de Abajo; *licenciado* Sanabria, the private secretary of the governor of the state of Mezcala; Congressman Medrano; one railway-union leader and two peasant leaders; the manager of the San Pedro de las Corrientes branch of the Mezcala Bank; a number of businessmen; and the proprietor of a stable of over a hundred cows. Two of the three mayors who were invited arrived at two A.M., immediately after having concluded officiating over the Independence Day ceremony in their respective townships. The Baladros had reached the pinnacle of their social career, a fact of which they were unaware since they considered that yet other heights remained for them to scale.

At midnight—the festivities started somewhat late—the doors of the balcony opened and Arcángela stepped out, a bell in her hand, together with *licenciado* Canales, who carried his country's flag. Arcángela rang the bell to attract the attention of those below and everybody applauded. When there was silence, *licenciado* Canales waved the flag and pronounced the following

50

version of the traditional Cry of Independence: "Long Live Mexico! Long live national independence! Long live the Heroes who won us our liberty! Long live the Baladro sisters! Long live the Casino del Danzón!"

Licenciado Canales's words were received with shouts of approval.

(This was the first incident. Congressman Medrano and one of the peasant leaders were of the opinion that *vivas* jointly for the national heroes and the Baladro sisters constituted blasphemous juxtaposition and brought word of the incident to the ears of Governor Cabañas who at once dismissed *licenciado* Canales from his post and broke off his friendship with him, thereby nullifying the only influence the Baladros had at the state house of Plan de Abajo.)

At the inaugural celebration, the Baladros, wearing evening gowns for the first time in their lives—Serafina describes her dress as iridescent—received their guests in the dining room of the house and not until all were together did they usher them into the cabaret. The decorations caused an unforgettable impression. When the exclamations had died down, the girls entered, nicely dressed and elegantly coiffed. Serafina chose this moment to announce that everything would be on the house for the evening. This statement gave rise to confusion: The guests took it to imply that "everything" included the girls, whereas the girls assumed it to mean that if nobody had to pay a check, they had no obligation to go to bed with anybody.

After the "Cry of Independence," witnesses say, Arcángela led the guests to the Baghdad Salon where the "show," in which three women participated, was presented for the first time. Several of the spectators became overexcited and would have incorporated themselves into the spectacle had Arcángela not stopped them.

When everybody had returned to the cabaret, the dancing began, and the second incident occurred.

What happened was this: *Licenciado* Sanabria, whom nobody had ever suspected of equivocal tendencies, was suddenly overcome by a murky passion and felt impelled to dance with Ladder, who had come into the cabaret to deliver a message. The two men danced a danzon

51

entitled "Nerëidas" from start to finish before the hor-
rified assemblage—nobody else dared to dance. At the
conclusion of the piece, Ladder thanked his partner and
left. *Licenciado* Sanabria then tried to dance with various other gentlemen who declined his invitation. He
realized, finally, that he had cut a sorry figure and held
a grudge ever after against all who had been witnesses
to his disgrace—and against the Baladros, in particular,
for having been instrumental in his succumbing to
temptation. This ill will was to play an important part
in the story, as will be seen later.

2

The snag was the following:

What got into Governor Cabañas that caused him to
do something that had never entered anybody's mind in
Plan de Abajo in one hundred forty years of indepen-
dent government—the banning of prostitution?

The motives suggested by the various explanations
for this mystery are like branches springing from a single root, which is that, of all the governors in the history of Plan de Abajo, Cabañas was the most ambitious
and stubborn. His predecessors, all provincial politi-
cians, were quite played out by the time they took office,
whereas Governor Cabañas came to the governorship
fresh and strongly motivated to push to new heights in
his career. This drive, coupled with the fact that the
country had not been governed by a native son of Plan
de Abajo in some one hundred and twenty years, kindled in him the idea that he was presidential timber.

He reorganized the state government along the lines
of a small-scale republic—the tax office was renamed
the Ministry of the Treasury, the board of improve-
ments became the Ministry of Public Works, and so
forth. And, he was bent on demonstrating that being
capable of governing the one so effectively he would certainly be just as capable of governing the other, if the
powers that be gave him the opportunity.

In addition to changing the names of the depart-ments, Cabañas embarked on a number of monumental public works—a state office building, a highway, and a tunnel—which cost an enormous amount of money and produced a deficit that Cabañas had to compensate for by raising taxes.

He wished to accomplish this in the form least painful to the taxpayers and, to that end, he organized "businessmen's colloquies." These consisted of the governor arriving in person at the various cities where he would meet with the businessmen of the area in the casino of each place for the purpose of demonstrating to them that the taxes they paid to the state were a pittance and that it was urgent for them to pay more. The businessmen responded to this call by pointing out that the state was a pigsty and not worth even what they were currently paying. They raised complaints about everything from the diameter of the sewer pipes and the insufficient water supply to the plague of centers of vice "to which the authorities shut their eyes."

As a result of the colloquies, Cabañas increased taxes, and to placate the disgruntled, at least partially— among the complaints brought up, he remedied the one that cost the least money—he decreed the closing down of houses of prostitution throughout the state.

The Plan de Abajo Morals Act, which bans prostitution and pandering, and brands as a lawbreaker even a person who delivers soft drinks to a brothel, was presented to the state congress under the sponsorship of Governor Cabañas, debated for half an hour, and passed unanimously to applause on March 2, 1962.

The enforcement of the law, something nobody anticipated, affected close to thirty thousand persons whose livelihood was directly or indirectly derived from prostitution, as well as the municipal governments, 30 to 40 percent of whose revenue came from the taxes paid by the brothels, and the hundreds of public employees who received gratuities from their proprietors. None of the affected parties put forward objections.

(It is known that Arcángela, accompanied by *licenciado* Rendón, appeared in Judge Peralta's office and offered him five thousand pesos for a writ of *amparo* that would protect her. The judge describes his reply as having been couched in the following words addressed to *licenciado* Rendón: "Try to make señora Baladro understand that what she is requesting me to grant her is not precisely an *amparo*, but rather a judicial instrument that would grant her immunity with respect to a law passed by congress. Explain to her, in addition, that even if what she is asking me for were an *amparo*, I would be unable to grant it to her at any price, in view of the fact that the governor has personally requested all judges not to hamper enforcement of this law, in which he has taken a particular interest.")

3

The Morals Act was enforced with a stringency unprecedented in the history of the state of Plan de Abajo. By the end of March, not a single brothel remained in operation.

Serafina and Arcángela Baladro, following what appears to have been prophetic intuition, removed the furniture from the Molino Street house but left the Casino del Danzón intact, with the beds made, on the day the inspectors came to paste the seals over the doors. The sisters say they had a premonition that very soon God was going to grant the miracle of making it possible for them to reopen the model brothel that was so dear to them.

Touching scenes were to be witnessed the day the Molino Street house in Pedrones was closed. Six trucks filled with furniture and women were lined up at the curb—three whorehouses in the one block. The farewells between some of the girls were quite moving, because the Baladros had disposed of eleven of them to an individual who had businesses in Guatáparo. The sidewalks were crowded with bystanders, people who had never set foot within a brothel but were curious to see what sorts of things had been inside. The policemen on duty kept their eyes averted and were in bad humor because they were losing a source of extra income. When *licenciado* Avalos arrived to affix the seals, he said to Serafina, "Please don't take it personally, doña Serafina. I am only doing this because it is my duty." She had been giving him five hundred pesos a month for the last four years.

When the seals had been pasted across the doors and the trucks loaded, one of the women who lived on the block came over to Serafina and thanked her in the name of the other neighbors for having paid for the installation of their sidewalks.

4

The girls, chairs, beds, basins, mattresses, and bundles of clothing in the trucks reached San Pedro de las Corrientes toward evening of what was a sad day. The proprietresses arrived by car in a foul mood.

The initial days were difficult, because twenty-six women had to be installed where fourteen had formerly lived and it was necessary to divide the rooms, which left them cramped. Besides, the contractor charged what seemed to Arcángela an outrageous price. She was quite downcast for several weeks, thinking that they were going to be left in poverty. This mood lasted until she made a deal with a señora Eugenia, who operated a business is Mezcala, to transfer another eight girls. This transaction, however, was never consummated because customers began to arrive. Some were former regulars from Plan de Abajo who crossed the state line in search of recreation; others were new and also from Plan de Abajo who, although not frequenters of whorehouses, succumbed to temptation on seeing them prohibited and shut down. The influx of outsiders in search of pleasures forbidden in other parts acted as a stimulus upon the San Pedro de las Corrientes males and impelled them to visit the cabarets more assiduously. "Men are like flies," Serafina observes, "the more they see lighting in a place, the more they want to light there, too."

The México Lindo was packed nightly. On Saturdays, there were not enough women to meet the demand. Serafina bought a new jukebox that she paid for herself. Seeing the Baladros become so prosperous in San Pedro de las Corrientes, Captain Bedoya put in for a transfer to another unit closer by. What bothered him most about his living in Concepción and Serafina in San Pedro was riding in the Scarlet Arrow buses twice a day —he became convinced that his life was going to come to a sudden end in an accident on Dog Hill. Arcángela took to saying that business had never been so good and that what God had taken away with one hand from her sister and herself, He was returning to them with the other. Then came December and the Humberto incident.

VII
A Life

1

The man comes down the hill, his shoulders drawn up, arms rigid, fists clenched, head twisted, legs now stiff now flaccid, feet finding the ground halfway there or losing contact with the surface, forcing him to take a step back. (Those who saw him go by, it was learned later on, thought he was drunk.)

It is nine o'clock at night. The way down from the Sanctuary is a steep cobblestone street with steps wherever needed, lined by two-story houses with painted walls and closed doors. There is a streetlight every hundred meters. The center of town is at the foot of the hill. Fireworks from the square light up the sky intermittently. A confusion of sounds is to be heard—sky rockets, brass bands, jukeboxes, mariachis, voices, howls of rustic gusto, yelping dogs. The date is the eighth of December.

The man's vitality is at too low an ebb for him to be aware of any of this; he holds his glazed eyes fixed on the ground, absorbed in reaching his goal. The dogs that watch him go by bark at him and then approach to sniff at the blood that had fallen. Following him, fifty meters above on the hill, are two detectives who stop each time he stops, clutching the trunk of a tree to catch his breath. The detectives move on when the man continues his dogged way.

He faces his sternest test when he reaches the foot of

the hill. He stops at the corner and, without raising his eyes, as though recognizing the stones of the street, turns to the right and goes along Allende Street, walking more slowly. The people watch him pass, stumble and bump into a wall, leaving a stain that will go unrecognized until the next day. "The dead man left a mark here with his blood," the people are to say, pointing out the blackish smear.

The man staggers, lurching from one foot to the other, loses his sense of direction, stumbles diagonally across the street to bump into a taco stand in a doorway, sending the table, brazier, burning charcoal, frying pan, plates, and tacos flying in all directions to fall clattering on the cobblestones. He continues on his way, his gait more uncontrolled the faster he moves. The people make way for him. The taco woman gives chase and catches up with him, but on seeing his ghastly pallor, before she can give vent to her outrage, falls silent and returns disconsolately to pick up the wreckage and recover her tacos.

The electric sign says "México Lindo." Making an agonizing effort, the man succeeds in negotiating the single step at the entrance, separates the panels of the little door, enters the smoke-filled cabaret, pushes two customers aside, leans on a table whose occupants stare, not recognizing him, overturns a drink, and drops to the floor.

The hum of conversation stops abruptly as a woman screams. The people crowd around. Automatically, the jukebox begins to blare a mambo. Somebody, sensibly, disconnects it. There is not a sound. Serafina, who is at the cash register, crosses the dance floor, pushing her way through the onlookers until she reaches the center of attention where she recognizes the corpse on the floor as her nephew.

2

There are as many gaps in what is known about the life of Humberto Paredes Baladro, Arcángela's son, as there are in what is known about his death.

He was born in the Molino Street house in 1939. Arcángela was his mother; his father a man on whom there is no information except that his family name was Paredes. (Arcángela pretends not to understand when questioned about this person.)

Serafina says that several months before Humberto was born, she met her sister in the market and noted that she was pregnant, but made no comment because she considered that "it would have been disrespectful." She did not know that Arcángela had given birth until she was invited to the christening. Serafina is sure that the child's mother did not mention his father then or anytime thereafter.

The boy grew up in the whorehouse, but his mother was determined to make a respectable man of him. The Skeleton says that Arcángela forbade him to go out into the patio, up the stairs, into the rooms, or to enter the yard. The girls were warned not to explain to the child why the men who came to the house were there. This discipline was so effective that Humberto Paredes was totally innocent when he entered school. On his first day, the other children, who knew who he was, gave him an education. When he came home, he asked the Skeleton, "Are you a whore?" The Skeleton said she was and when the boy wanted to know if his mother was one, too, she answered that, no, she was a madam.

On his third day of school, the principal heard a chorus of rhythmic shouts coming from the yard and when she went out to see what was happening, she found thirty children running and jumping up and down in circles "like redskins" and shouting, "son of a whore!" In the center was the pupil, Paredes Baladro, crying.

Humberto was sent home, accompanied by the watchman, with an envelope containing thirty pesos, the fee Arcángela had paid for his registration, and a note from the principal requesting the child's mother to send him to another school.

After she had read the note Arcángela realized that the time had come when she and her son had to part. In order to isolate him from any contact with vice, she enrolled him in schools in places far away where nobody would know his mother's name or suspect what her profession was.

During this period, Arcángela wrote him long weekly letters in green ink on ruled paper filled with advice, such as to smear lard behind his ears to protect him from catching cold, to sleep with his feet pointing south to avoid the evil eye, and so on. The only copies of these that survive are a few her son had discarded and which remained forgotten among his belongings. His replies were short requests for money, which had no effect—where Arcángela got the idea that money is the worst corruptor of youth is not known—but she preserves them to this day in a lacquered box of scented wood from Olinalá.

The boy changed boarding schools on a number of occasions. The first time was when the superintendent of the Ignacio Allende School in Muerdago discovered two holes in the bathroom used by his wife. As reported by various of the students on being questioned, the holes, which had been made in the wall of a little-used corridor, were the work of the student Paredes Baladro—twelve years of age—who was charging his schoolmates fifty centavos for a look at the superintendent's wife in the bathtub and twenty centavos sitting on the toilet.

A year later, several of the boys at the Juan Escutia School complained to the office that they were being shaken down by the student Paredes Baladro. He was extorting one peso per week from each one and if anybody did not pay he had him beaten up by the student Gutiérrez Carrasco, alias "the Gorilla."

It is also known that he entered medical school in Cuévano but did not complete the first year. His studies came to an abrupt end the day he stabbed a classmate—it is not known for what reason. The incident took place in one of the classrooms. The police were called in and a nasty situation developed. Arcángela had to intervene. She paid the medical expenses as well as a large settlement to the victim's family—luckily, they turned out to be poor and amenable to reason—for withdrawing charges. Arcángela bought off witnesses, bought the judge, and did not rest until he was free. *Licenciado* Rendón convinced her that it would be best for Humberto to go to the United States until the scandal blew over.

Humberto Paredes spent a year in Los Angeles. His

mother hoped he would learn English and that with this
asset he would be able to establish himself in business.
She was mistaken only by half. Humberto returned to
San Pedro de las Corrientes without knowing how to
speak a word of English, but he did bring back poppy
seeds that were to give him a source of income during
the few years of life remaining to him.

Humberto Paredes continued living at the México
Lindo, but under instructions from the people he
worked for, it seems, he rented a house on Los Bridones
Street. There, ostensibly, he dealt in seeds, but the
house actually must have been where he cached the narcotics and conducted his transactions. It should be
pointed out, however, that the police found nothing
compromising there after Humberto's death nor were
they able to learn who his contacts were.

3

In each of the three extant photographs of him, Humberto Paredes reveals the wide, flat face and square jaw
inherited from his mother, the lank hair of the Indian,
and the sneering lip of the autocrat—a kind of Benito
Juárez of the underworld.

In the first photograph, the subject appears at the
wheel of a Buick convertible—blood-red, according to
those who had seen it—which he bought out of the proceeds of his first deal, and the only luxury he ever
possessed in his life. There is a huisache tree in the
background. In the second photograph, he is in profile,
wearing a striped sweater. He is gripping in his right
hand the .38 pistol found on him when he was killed.
Arcángela maintains, nevertheless, that she never saw
her son use a firearm. The wall that can be seen at the
rear in this shot is undoubtedly that of the México
Lindo. In the third photograph, Humberto appears in
swimming trunks, his hair wet. He is looking into the
camera and smiling, his arm clasping the waist of a village belle who is wearing a spectacular bathing suit and
a bunch of artificial ringlets.

61

She says that she had seen him before, in his red car, and that she had a bad impression of him because it seemed to her that "he was only interested in attracting attention"—Humberto wore a red shirt and green eyeglasses, made the exhaust of his car roar, blew the horn constantly, and so on. She was crossing the street one day when he appeared in his car and veered sharply, nearly knocking her down. Seeing that he had frightened her, he stopped, and instead of apologizing, opened the door and invited her to get in. Offended, she continued on her way. He followed in the car, keeping pace with her, but without proffering the sort of comments that men customarily make to women under such circumstances. This seemed strange to her. He continued behind her as far as the hill of the Sanctuary, where there is no thoroughfare. When he saw her start up the slope, he parked the car and followed her at a distance on foot, making no effort to catch up with her and "without calling out vulgar remarks or trying to get close enough to put his hands on me." She reached home, entered, closed the door, went upstairs to her room and looked out the window in time to see him stand in front of the house, hesitate a moment, and then start down the hill. In the days that followed she mentioned his name to various girl friends who repeated to her what they had heard about him: that he was the son of a procuress; had stabbed a boy when he was still in school; had been in jail and had to leave the country until things blew over; was a drug dealer—besides other imagined crimes imputed to him.

Federal narcotics agent Demetrio Guillomar arrived in Pedrones with orders to find out who the middleman was between the poppy growers of the region and those who processed the gum, and to obtain the evidence necessary to bring him to trial. Since it was suspected that this middleman was being protected by the local authorities, Guillomar had instructions not to contact them or make known the reason for his presence. He registered at the Hotel Frances as an insurance salesman and after spending several fruitless weeks in the area, he suddenly learned something. How, is not exactly known. Possibly, Bedoya's trail—he had discovered the plantations and burned them out—led him to Humberto Paredes, whose name appears in the federal police records for the first time on November 15, 1962, in a report by Guillomar.

She says she suffered a great deal; that she could not decide whether to believe what people said about Humberto or what her heart told her—that nobody as sweet as he could be bad. She still has the clay pitcher from Cuevano with the words "True Love" on it that he gave her. She did not accept when he invited her for a ride or to have ice cream with him in Muerdago because, in the first place, it was an open car and she might be seen and, secondly, because she thought that getting into a car with a boy meant losing her virginity, which she had made up her mind to maintain intact until marriage. In view of these obstacles, the couple had no choice but to stroll, conversing, along the paths by the river, which are wooded and solitary. On these walks, Humberto told her things about his life that did not jibe with what people said about him and Conchita therefore wondered whether he was telling the truth or deceiving her. She talked to him of the future, her ideas about marriage, how many children she planned to have, what she was going to name them, and how she would bring them up. She did not suspect that these conversations exasperated him, until the day he took her firmly by the arm, led her down an embankment, dumped her on the ground, and tore her panties off. Having accomplished this disconcerted Humberto momentarily, which Conchita took advantage of to run away. He did not pursue her. The following day, Humberto waited for her at a spot where he knew she would have to pass—Conchita was a teacher at a parochial school—and begged her pardon. She told him she never wanted to see him again.

Detective Guillomar made several trips to San Pedro de las Corrientes and had talks with Humberto Paredes. It is even possible that the agent pretended that he wanted to sell a poppy crop or buy opium. Or, perhaps, he made no pretense at all and simply admitted who he was. There is a strong probability that the ten thousand pesos Humberto withdrew from the bank on December 1, found their way into Detective Guillomar's pocket. Apparently, Humberto had his last opportunity to escape in the days that followed, but did not take advantage of it.

She says that, worn out by his persistence, she consented to go to the resort at El Farallón Lake with him on the condition that they make the trip by bus and not in his car, but when it turned out that all the seats had been sold they went in the car after all, and that Humberto treated her with consideration, making no attempt to take advantage of her. The snapshot of them that survives was taken there by a photographer. They spent a wonderful day. When they returned to San Pedro de las Corrientes, as he was opening the door of the car for her, her two brothers passed by. Conchita says that for a moment she was afraid that they were going to confront Humberto—she had been forbidden to go out with him—but they went on their way without even turning around, as though they had not noticed anything. This is what she thought, but when she got home, they were there, waiting for her, in a rage. They reprimanded her severely and warned her not to see him again.

"He is a dead man if he ever comes near you again," one of her brothers said to her.

Later, Conchita saw them take pistols out of a drawer and oil them.

On December 7, federal agent Pacheco arrived in Pedrones, met Guillomar, and delivered instructions to him to make the arrest.

She says that on the morning of the eighth, her saint's day, a stranger knocked on the door—probably Ticho, from the description—and delivered a gift-wrapped package sent by Humberto Paredes. Conchita refused to accept it. She had decided that it would be wiser not to see Humberto anymore because of her brothers.

Detectives Guillomar and Pacheco were on the point of arresting Humberto Paredes as he was coming out of El Galeón bar with a group of mariachis at seven o'clock in the evening. They did not do so because of the possibility that the musicians were his friends and might put up resistance. They decided to wait and followed at a distance as they climbed the Sanctuary hill.

She says that when she heard the mariachis playing "Heartless Woman" she felt distraught. She knew the piece was being played for her and that Humberto had brought the serenade. She would have liked to go out and warn Humberto to go away, that her brothers were home and had guns, but she could not leave the house because she had to entertain some visitors who had come to congratulate her. She says that the mariachis played several pieces—"Perfidy," among others—and that the visitors asked her snidely, "Who do you suppose the serenade could be for, Conchita?"

She says that she saw her brothers leave the living room and go out to the patio. That shortly after the mariachis finished playing the final piece, she looked out the window and saw them walking down the hill without Humberto and that then she heard a knock on the door and, not being able to stand it any longer, decided to go out and see what was happening. As she was walking downstairs she heard the shots. (It appears that the Zamora brothers, lurking behind some flowerpots, opened the door by pulling on the cord attached to the bolt, and shot the person standing on the threshold, who was Humberto.)

Detectives Guillomar and Pacheco followed the man they were going to arrest at a distance as he went down the hill and along Allende Street. When they saw him enter the México Lindo they alerted the policeman, Segoviano, who was standing on the corner.

VIII
The Bad Night

1

One of the girls leaves the cabaret to notify the mother. The moment she is out of the room the scene freezes like a tableau on a stage. Everybody stares spellbound at the corpse, some moving only to obtain a better vantage point. There is absolute silence.

Suddenly a whistle blast is heard. It is Segoviano, the policeman, making known his presence on the corner. The trance is instantly shattered. Fascinated and respectful contemplation turns into panic. The sound of the whistle reminds the clientele of the existence of the police and impels them toward the exit. Stampeding, they tear the doors off their hinges, breaking out the frames; they reach the street and disperse, the more circumspect walking rapidly without turning their heads until they reach the square. The tumult over, Segoviano enters the cabaret, finding only the girls, the waiters, and the corpse inside. He blows another blast on his whistle and barks, "Nobody move! Lock all the doors!"

What follows lies between pathos and tedium. While the police doctor and the authorities are being awaited, the mother, who was in her room doing accounts, enters the cabaret to see what is going on—she was told of something terrible having happened, but they did not dare to say what—and on recognizing the dead body on the floor as that of her son she emits strange shrieks, inarticulate guttural cries, the like of which no one had ever heard before or will hear again. She does not approach the body, does not take it in her arms, or contemplate it wracked with sobs, as might be expected, but moves backward away from it, sits on the edge of a chair and, with her hands resting on her knees, closes her eyes and howls.

The Department of Justice representative asks questions for the record: "Where were you when you heard the shots?" "I did not hear any shots." "Then how did you know anything out of the ordinary was happening?" "I saw a dead body on the floor" and so forth and so on.

It is late when the police doctor appears, wearing a hat and muffler—he has a cold—sets his satchel on the floor and takes the corpse's pulse. He then goes to the telephone, calls for an ambulance, picks up the satchel, and goes home.

The women light candles and set them around Humberto. They cover his face—he is lying on his back—with a blue silk kerchief. The ambulance attendants arrive with a stretcher, put the body on it—knocking over two of the candles—and carry it out. There is a large crowd on the street despite the lateness of the hour. The agent carries on with his questioning: "And what did you see?"

2

Humberto Paredes's wake was held in absentia. While his body lay in the municipal hospital on a slab waiting to be autopsied, the weeping women, dressed in black, gathered in the dining room, put the table in a corner, lighted candles, knelt, and recited prayers led by the Skeleton, who had been devout as a girl. Arcángela did not attend the wake. She spent the night alone in her room in the dark, quiet and half-dazed, thanks to a potion of boiled lettuce leaves the Skeleton had given her to drink. Captain Bedoya, who was notified by Serafina, arrived in San Pedro de las Corrientes on the last Scarlet Arrow bus, entered the dining room in the middle of the Lord's Prayer, removed his cap, and kneeling on one knee, crossed himself, something he rarely did, being an atheist. After an interval, realizing that the deceased was not there, he sat down.

At ten o'clock the following morning, Serafina, accompanied by Captain Bedoya and *licenciado* Rendón, requested permission from the mayor's office to remove her nephew's body from the municipal hospital. The mayor, a friend of hers, broke the news to her: An order had arrived to close the México Lindo. Serafina was thunderstruck, but Captain Bedoya and *licenciado* Rendón, between them, succeeded in convincing her that what the mayor had said could not be correct because it would be a violation of the state constitution.

The inspector arrived with the official notice at four o'clock in the afternoon, just as the undertakers were removing the coffin from the house. Permission to Arcángela to operate the México Lindo was canceled indefinitely for violation of the health regulations of the state of Mezcala: The dimensions of the windows in the men's toilets were eighteen inches square instead of a minimum of twenty, as provided by law. The owner was given twenty-four hours to vacate the premises.

When Arcángela signed at the bottom of the document in acknowledgment of its receipt, she was not aware of what she was doing. Grief had left her deranged. *Licenciado* Rendón was notified of this turn of events by Serafina and he promised to obtain a stay.

During the funeral procession, the hearse broke down. The cemetery chaplain, Father Grajales, refused to pronounce the customary oration because he considered the deceased a sinner who had never given any indication of repentance. Arcángela fainted at the moment the gravediggers threw the first shovelful of earth into the grave.

3

When the mourners returned from the cemetery at six o'clock in the evening, they met *licenciado* Rendón, who informed them that no judge in town was willing to grant a stay. Upon entering the México Lindo, they saw that Judge Torres had set up a temporary office in the cabaret. A notary public and two stenographers were with him. The judge separated the girls from the Baladro sisters and had them go into the cabaret and sit on chairs he had purposely placed on the far side of the room where they were to wait their turn and come one by one to the other end where he, the notary public, and the stenographers were. The judge asked his questions in a low voice and instructed each girl to answer in a low voice also so as not to influence the others or give them time to prepare answers. After having replied to the judge's questions, each one left the cabaret.

The questions the judge asked the girls were: For how long had they been practicing prostitution; how long while working for the Baladro sisters; if they had been mistreated; and if they had exercised the profession voluntarily or under coercion by another person.

The twenty-six who replied said that they had not been mistreated and that they practiced prostitution voluntarily. The questioning was carried on in such a way as to encourage the girls to tell the truth. This is a point of interest, in view of the fact that fourteen months later, various of those who had been questioned stated exactly the opposite.

The original record of this testimony may be examined in the files of the San Pedro de las Corrientes courthouse.

(Three irregularities concerning the death of Humberto Paredes Baladro are evident in the records: The official document prepared by the attorney general's office gives the impression that the deceased died as a consequence of a shooting inside the México Lindo, despite the fact that nobody present stated that he had heard shots; the Zamora brothers were never brought to trial; federal agents Guillomar and Pacheco admitted having followed the person they had orders to arrest down the hill, but did not say that they could see that he was dying. There is no indication that the authorities found any evidence in the México Lindo or the house on Los Bridones Street to show that Humberto Paredes Baladro was involved in the drug traffic.)

That night, in the dining room, Serafina discussed with Captain Bedoya what would have to be done the following day in order to vacate the house. Arcángela, apparently, took no part in this conversation.

Captain Bedoya asserts that in view of the fact that all the houses belonging to the sisters were now closed, he advised Serafina to dismiss the employees and devote herself to some other activity.

He says that Serafina refused to take his advice for two reasons: First, because a judge was now involved and he would unquestionably compel her to give each dismissed girl separation pay; second, *licenciado* Rendón was going to take legal steps to revoke the closure order since he considered that shutting the México Lindo was unjustified and certainly not final, and had promised her that in two months' time—or three, at the most—she and her sister would be reopening.

After dismissing the idea of getting rid of the girls, Serafina and the captain discussed what to do with them until the México Lindo was back in operation. They considered various possibilities, from that of putting up the twenty-six women at a hotel, which was rejected because of the expense, to that of distributing them among various whorehouses of the region, which Serafina vetoed because of the risk that the hospitable brothel keepers might refuse to return them later on. The solution finally adopted was illegal but very simple: to move out of one closed-down whorehouse into another closed-down whorehouse. They decided to take the girls to the Casino del Danzón, which had fifteen rooms and all the conveniences, where they could spend two or three months without anybody being the wiser. The seals would not have to be broken because they could enter the building by crossing over from the roof of the house next door, which belonged to señora Aurora Benavides, a kindhearted lady who would be incapable of refusing the Baladros a favor.

Aurora Bautista relates that Serafina called the girls together in the hall and said to them: "We will all be leaving this place tonight. Take with you only what you are wearing. Leave everything else in your rooms. We will be returning in two months."

No matter how much the girls insisted, she refused to say where she was taking them.

Captain Bedoya says that it was Ladder's idea that he, Bedoya, should sit next to the window in the car wearing his uniform cap with its three bars to impress the highway police in case the sight of five cars loaded with women passing one after another should attract attention and they were stopped.

Aurora Bautista states that she was sitting in the car next to Ladder outside the México Lindo when the captain came over, opened the door, and sat on top of her.

Captain Bedoya reports that the trip was uncomfortable but uneventful; however, that when they reached Concepción and got to Independence Street, they had to knock on the door of number 83 for nearly an hour before señora Benavides woke up and let them in.

Aurora Bautista says that she saw Serafina give Captain Bedoya money from her purse, which he distributed among the taxi drivers, warning them: "Forget everything you saw tonight. If you don't, then you better remember this, too." And he put his hand on the butt of the pistol hanging from his belt.

Captain Bedoya says that it was one of the most precarious moments of his life when he had to make the leap from one roof to the other holding Arcángela by the hand, because she was refusing to jump. They nearly plummeted to the ground together.

Aurora Bautista says that when they got to the Casino del Danzón there was no electricity, they had no candles, and nobody had brought any food. They went to sleep in the dark, two in a bed. The next morning, Ticho jumped across to the other roof and went to the market. They finally ate at two o'clock in the afternoon.

That day, December 10, 1962, señora Aurora Benavides and señora Serafina Baladro made an oral agreement in accordance with which the former would permit Eustiquio Natera (Ticho) to break through the wall between the vestibule of her house and the dining room of the Baladro house so as to permit persons in number 85 Independence Street to have access to number 83 without having to jump across the roofs. In consideration for this favor, señora Baladro agreed to pay señora Benavides the sum of two hundred pesos on the first day of each month.

Another agreement was also made on that date in accordance with which señora Benavides would permit the said Eustiquio Natera to connect a wire to her electrical service in order to pass current to the house next door. Twenty pesos.

Both agreements were kept by the two parties for the thirteen months that elapsed between the time they were entered into and the day Captain Teódulo Cueto found the bodies buried in the yard.

IX
The Secret Life

1

All the buildings of any importance in Concepción are located around the square: the town hall, the court-house, the police department, and the Gómez Hotel. Thirty-eight laurel trees grow in the square and are considered by many to be the town's most attractive feature; the churches, everybody agrees, are nothing at all. A gardener prunes these trees five times a year to maintain their perfectly cylindrical form, in imitation of the ones in Constitution Gardens in Cuévano, the state capital.

Concepción, which consists of only forty-two square blocks, is small. One cannot walk more than four blocks in any direction without coming to garbage dumps. The telephone directory lists twenty-eight subscribers in Concepción, of whom eleven are named Gómez.

A person standing on any of the streets that face east or south sees in perspective the adobe walls, the dirt roadway, and, against the horizon, the alfalfa fields. If, on the other hand, he looks west or north, he sees the hazy blue profile of the Güemes Mountains over the flat rooftops. Whoever strolls about town will note that all the doors are the same, of mesquite wood, and all the windows, of iron, are different, having been forged by a local blacksmith who took pride in never repeating a design.

Apart from the laurel trees and the windows, there is

nothing that distinguishes the town. It does not even produce the candied fruits that are sold there. They are brought in from Murángato.

There are four two-story buildings in Concepción: the town hall, the Gómez Hotel, the Casino del Danzón, and señora Benavides's house. The first two were built at the same time and inaugurated in 1910 during the Independence Centennial. Fifty years went by without a single inhabitant of Concepción having felt the need for a second floor, until the Baladro sisters arrived and built the Casino del Danzón. When its construction was at the halfway point, señora Benavides decided to add another story to her house, not because she needed more space—she is a widow and lives alone—but because she could not tolerate the idea of anybody in the same block having a house taller than hers.

Independence Street is the second block from the edge of town. On the corner nearest the Casino del Danzón there are a tortilla-dough mill and a butcher shop. Across the street and closer to it there is a small general store. The proprietors of these three businesses were aware that the girls had returned. None of them notified the police.

2

The neighbors noted signs of habitation in the Casino del Danzón between December 10, 1962 and the middle of January, 1964.

A woman living in the adjoining house states that she frequently heard voices in the rear yard and the sound of clothes being washed, and, one time, several women singing "Cooey, Cooey, Little Dove."

A boy states that one afternoon he decided to jump over the wall—of what he thought was an unoccupied house—to gather some of the avocados that had fallen to the ground. As he straddled the wall, he saw two women who had beaten him to it, bending over the fruit.

An employee of the electric light and power company states that every time he passed through Independence Street of an evening, it surprised him to see a light in

by the week: in the first column, their names; in the next two, "credits"—what each girl earned in commissions in the cabaret and from the work in her room; the next four, "debits"—the amounts deducted for room, board, clothing, and advances in cash. In the last columns, the weekly balances appear which, if negative, bear interest at the rate of 3 percent per month. During the months they lived in the closed-down Casino del Danzón without income, the girls piled up an enormous debt. The total came to over half a million pesos. Arcángela kept exact accounts of what each employee owed her until the middle of September, when she lost hope of ever collecting.)

In February—the Skeleton continues—señora Arcángela said that she could not go on supporting so many idle bitches and decided to sell eleven of the girls to don Sirenio Pantoja, who ran businesses in Jaloste and had said to her some time ago that he would take any girls she couldn't use off her hands. To tell the truth, the señora unloaded the worst of the lot on don Sirenio—the homeliest and the most unmanageable ones. We were much happier after they were gone. They say don Sirenio paid the señora eleven thousand pesos for them.

4

Licenciado Rendón, representing the Baladro sisters, instituted the following legal actions: three consecutive suits against public officials to establish that the closing of the México Lindo was unconstitutional, unfair, and inapplicable. He lost them all because the presiding judge found that *they* were inapplicable. *Licenciado* Rendón then requested the court to set the amount of the fine his clients would have to pay to reopen the México Lindo. The court deliberated so long with respect to the fine that this story will be over before its decision is announced.

Seeing that time was going by fruitlessly, *licenciado* Rendón applied for a license on behalf of his clients to open another business under a different name. The application was rejected on the grounds that payment by the applicants of the fine on the México Lindo was still pending. That is to say, they could not open a new business because they had not paid the fine and they could not pay the fine because they were not told how much it was. The judge would accept no bond or deposit. Finally, *licenciado* Rendón prepared a letter directly to the governor signed by the Baladros. Studded with courteous formalities, it requested that he grant them permission to open a nightclub "in any city of the state your honor should see fit to designate." This document made the slow transit from office to office until, finally, it came back to *licenciado* Rendón several months later with a handwritten notation in the margin: "Deny all requests from the signatories." This appeared over the signature of the governor's private secretary, *licenciado* Isidoro Sanabria—the man who danced with Ladder.

The legal steps taken by the Baladros in Plan de Abajo were more effective. In March, 1963, the restriction on the Molino Street house was lifted and it was sold to a leather-goods merchant who turned it into a workshop. Captain Bedoya was able to convince the sisters that the proceeds from this transaction should be invested in a farm.

5

My name is Radomiro Reyna Razo. I am a native of Concepción. I am the person who sold Los Pirules farm to the Baladro sisters, and I would like to point out that when I signed the deed I had no idea who they were or what line of business they were in and I certainly never imagined what they were going to do on the property I sold them.

What happened was this: I had to pay back a loan and did not have the money, so I decided to sell off part of my properties. I made this intention known to a number of people and, one day, Captain Bedoya, whom I knew by sight, came over to me in the bar of the Gómez Hotel and said to me, "How much commission will you pay if I get you a buyer for that land you are interested in selling?"

I made him an offer, he accepted, and two days later the señoras Baladro arrived at my house in a taxi.

Nobody would ever have taken them for procuresses. On the contrary, they looked so respectable that I invited them into my living room and introduced them to my wife. They were dressed in black. The older one, who had the greater authority, wore a shawl, as if she were going to spend the rest of the afternoon in church. She kept an eye on her sister as if she were a maiden. When the younger one crossed her leg, the older one said, "Serafina, cover yourself." And the other one tugged on her skirt until she got it down over her knee.

They made such a good impression on my wife that she served them vermouth and cookies, which they accepted. They drank in a very refined way and did not get drunk or use foul language. Then, I offered to drive them out to the property and my wife came along. Who would ever have believed that we were riding, my wife and I, in the same car with two procuresses?

The day we signed the deed, they arrived at the notary's office carrying a brown paper bag with grease stains on it out of which they took fifty thousand pesos in five-hundred-peso bills that they handed over to me. Captain Bedoya was present but he made a sign to me not to pay him his commission in front of the señoras. We went outside on some pretext and I gave him the money.

After the signing, when they and the captain had left, the notary, who knew who they were, told me what kind of women I had been dealing with. But, it was too late, the papers were already signed, I had the money in my hand, and I really needed it.

6

Eulalia Baladro de Pinto states:

Teófilo had just lost everything we had in the world for the third time. When my sisters' letter arrived, the *licenciados* were attaching the living room furniture. The letter said:

Dear Eulalia,

Since the business that has been giving us our livelihood for so many years is getting more and more troublesome all the time to operate, we have decided to go in for farming. We would like Teófilo, who knows so much about farms, to manage ours for us . . . (etc.)

The letter was written by Arcángela but signed by the two of them. Teófilo and I saw a ray of hope in this and the next day we packed our things and went to Concepción. (She states that they stopped at the Gómez Hotel on her sisters' instructions. She claims that in the seven months that followed, during which they had frequent dealings with them, neither she nor her husband had any idea that they were both living in the Casino del Danzón. In the afternoon of the same day they arrived they went in Ladder's car with the two sisters to see the farm.)

"I want you to plant flowers on this piece of ground," Arcángela said to Teófilo, "to put on Humberto's grave on the Day of the Dead."

It was the beginning of the rainy season and the corn was sprouting—Eulalia says—but the place seemed very desolate to me. (She describes the farmhouse, the ruined barn, the shed falling to pieces, and the depression that gripped her when, as she looked around, she realized there was not another inhabited house as far as the eye could see.)

Teófilo drew up a plan—Eulalia explains—of what had to be done on the farm to make it productive and estimated what it would cost. The plan sounded good to my sisters but they considered the price very high. They gave my husband less than half the money he needed, and in dribs and drabs. He was able to fix up the house with that amount but not to connect the water or electricity. He managed to repair the barn, but there was no money to buy cows and he could plant corn but not alfalfa. And, in place of essentials, they gave us something we did not need: One morning, my sisters arrived at the farm with a long package wrapped in newspapers. Arcángela put it on the kitchen table and told Teófilo to open it. It was a rifle.

"I brought it for you," she said to Teófilo, "to use on anybody who tries to steal our cows."

There weren't any cows ever, then or later.

7

On July 14, the Baladro sisters made a picnic on Los Pirules farm. They invited a priest to bless the land just purchased and to baptize it with its new name—formerly, it was called El Pitayo. The list of guests who attended the picnic reflects the change in the Baladro fortunes. Instead of local congressmen, mayors, labor leaders, and bank managers, those present were Captain Bedoya, a subaltern of his by the name of Brave Nicolás, Ladder, Ticho, and Teófilo Pinto. Fifteen girls were also there. While they were waiting for the priest to arrive, the men and women formed teams and got up a soccer game with a ball Ladder had in the trunk of his car.

After the priest had gone—to officiate at a christening—the guests opened bottles and toasted the occasion. The food was served late—red *mole* prepared by the Skeleton, the rice by Eulalia—Ladder played the guitar and the girls sang. It did not rain.

Three days later, Blanca died.

X
The Story of Blanca

(Blanca X: b. Ticomán, 1936—d. Concepción, 1963)

1

The sand in Ticomán is white and soft and your feet
sink into it as you walk. The beach is wide. A stony
creek flows by it into the sea. As far back as memory
goes, the natives have dug wells in the bed of this creek
during the dry season. The Ticomán people are inlan-
ders and ignore the sea. The men work corn patches on
the slopes of the hill, the women feed the pigs in the cor-
rals. Nobody knows how to swim, nobody would venture
into the sea, nobody expects anything from it. All that
they make use of from the sea is the driftwood. They
wait for the branches to be swept into the sea by the
creek during the rainy season and for the waves to cast
them up on the beach.

Two white cliffs can be seen in the distance in this neglected part of the ocean and, beyond, ships that pass
without ever stopping at Ticomán.

The families are large. When the adult males get
drunk they talk about going elsewhere to work. When
the male children grow up, they leave. The females re-
main, but not all of them.

One can imagine Blanca as a little girl doing what the

other children of her age in Ticomán did: walking along
the beach with a dog, gathering driftwood at the edge of
the sea, drawing water from the well—until an old
woman who wore a shawl took to sitting in a rush chair
and looking out to sea. She saw the child pass by carrying an armful of driftwood.

The story now moves from the beach to the annual
fair in Ocampo. Many devout people come to this fair to
keep their vows to the Virgin of Ocampo. Some carry
heavy beams on their backs from the hermitage, where
the spring of miraculous water is; others walk barefoot
over a stretch of cactus leaves; women crawl on their
knees across the atrium of the church, which has a
pumice-stone floor one hundred meters wide. The object
is to arrive bleeding before the holy image; only in this
way can one be sure of forgiveness or that the miracle
one has prayed for will be granted.

Many attend this fair not out of religious motives but
for its commercial activity. A great variety of things
are bought and sold: incense, Easter tapers, silver votive offerings, horses, fighting cocks, a team of oxen, a
woman.

At the 1950 Ocampo fair, Jovita X, the old woman who
sat in the rush-bottom chair looking out to sea in the
afternoons, sold a fourteen-year-old girl named Blanca
to Arcángela and Serafina Baladro for three hundred
pesos.

According to the Skeleton, who was a witness to the
transaction, it took place in one of the sheds in Ocampo
in which the pilgrims are put up. The Baladros inspected the child thoroughly before closing the deal and
found no defect other than discolored teeth—everybody's teeth are discolored in Ticomán because of the
water they drink from the wells in the creek bed—
which became a bargaining point. Señora Jovita was
asking four hundred pesos.

Something else took place that day which, as the
Skeleton recalled many years later, had all the ear-
marks of a bad omen. What happened was this: A pair
of sisters came to the same eating place where the Baladros had their meals while they were in Ocampo. They
were with their father, who was fulfilling a vow. Sera-

83

fina, on the lookout for girls for the Molino Street house, noticed that these two were pretty and, taking advantage of a moment when their father was not there, she struck up a conversation with them. She told them that she owned a shoe store in Pedrones and needed salesgirls. She offered them room and board and two hundred pesos a month. The prospect of going to live in Pedrones apparently appealed to the girls and they promised to give Serafina an answer the next day —that is to say, the day the Baladros bought Blanca. After having closed the deal and paid for her, they took her to the restaurant. The four of them—the Skeleton was the fourth—were on the second course, the rice, when the man who was keeping the vow arrived accompanied this time not by his two daughters but by two policemen who hauled Serafina off. She was held in the municipal jail for twenty-four hours on the charge of attempted corruption of minors. Arcángela had to pay two hundred and fifty pesos to get her out. The omen, the Skeleton explains, was that Blanca's first day with them ended in the first night Serafina spent in a jail.

2

Blanca's character:

Even though she was separated from her family under false pretenses, sold for a price, and initiated into prostitution at the age of fourteen, everything seems to indicate that she was happy.

It is not known what señora Jovita might have promised Blanca—or what she promised the mother and the mother promised Blanca—that induced her to accompany her for four hundred kilometers, the distance between Ticomán and Ocampo. Most likely, however, the promise was not kept. Nevertheless, when the deception was out in the open and the Baladros were inspecting Blanca amidst the cots in the pilgrims' shed, she showed no signs of surprise or embarrassment, the Skeleton says admiringly, and accompanied the Baladros without a word when señora Jovita told her to "go along with the señoras," nor was her appetite affected when the policemen took Serafina, she being the only one who ate the dessert. Several days later at the México Lindo when Arcángela was explaining what her duties would be—the moment, according to the Skeleton, when many begin to cry—she said impassively, "Whatever you say, señora." In all Blanca's years as a prostitute, the Skeleton recalls many compliments for her, but not a single word of complaint.

She used various names, being listed in the State of Mezcala Venereal Disease Registry as María de Jesús Gómez, María Elena Lara, Pilar Cardona, Norma Mendoza and, finally, under the name she kept until her death and by which she is remembered to this day: Blanca Medina. (The only reason she did not carry on the practice of changing her name any further, the Skeleton observes, was not because she wouldn't have liked to, but because Dr. Arellano, who was in charge of the registry, became annoyed and told her quite angrily that this name-changing of hers had to stop.)

The reason she assumed such a variety of names seems to be related to certain aspects of her personality which, despite its simplicity, had many facets. Those who knew her say that her great talent and the secret of her success lay in her capacity to instantly project qualities that each man expected, without his realizing it. This explains the contradictions in the accounts given by her admirers. She made one of them wait for her at the bar, alone, while she sat at a table, also alone, making believe that she was waiting for "a suitor" who did not exist and, of course, never arrived. Finally, feigning vindictiveness toward this man, she summoned the one at the bar, took him to her room and delivered herself in a kind of erotic catalepsy that he considered sensational. In contrast, with another man—a lawyer—she tore his necktie in the act of undressing him, pushed him violently back on the bed, and threw herself on top of him. He, likewise, was a satisfied customer.

Some say she was an attentive listener who patiently heard out all the stories she was told no matter how long-winded they were. Others describe her as talk-

ative. The Whoremaster, for example, says that each
time he visited her over a period of several months, she
related a new episode in a story she had made up. What
most impressed the Whoremaster, however, was that
simultaneously Blanca was telling a completely different story, also made up, to a friend of his who was fre-
quenting her during this same period. On the other
hand, a mining engineer who had been with Blanca just
once relates that they had a memorable tussle lasting a
couple of hours during which she did not utter a word.

The other girls with whom she worked remember her
with admiration and affection. Although she earned
more than any of them, she aroused no envy. She would
recommend the services of her less-favored companions, and if a good opportunity presented itself, she
would not hesitate to stand aside. Nobody can recall her
ever getting into a hair-pulling match with any of the
girls out of jealousy or greed. She gave away clothing to
the others that was still in good condition. The Baladros
and the Skeleton adored her.

It is known that Blanca felt inhibited about only one
thing, her discolored teeth. This prompted her acquisi-
tion of the only luxury she ever permitted herself. After
saving for years, she went to the best dentist in Pedrones who replaced her four upper incisors with gold
teeth. Although Blanca's appearance must have been
changed by this innovation, it does not seem to have dis-
figured her at all. According to the Whoremaster, who
knew her with her discolored teeth, without them—
while she was waiting for the new ones to be put in—
and with her gold teeth, he was not sure which way he
liked her best. The glitter of gold only accentuated her
exotic beauty: Blanca was black.

3

This is the story Blanca told the Whoremaster:

Blanca says that one day while she was out for a stroll
she sat down on a bench in the square. A man whom she

thought very handsome walked by, and then he walked by again, and then again. Finally the man sat down on a bench across from hers and kept looking at her. Blanca went back to the house without his having ventured to speak to her. The next day, Blanca returned to the square and the same man passed back and forth, ending up by sitting down and looking at her again. On the third day, he approaches her, tells her he is a professional soccer player, and wants to know who she is. She tells him she is a waitress in a restaurant. He proposes marriage. She tells him that would be impossible because she has an invalid mother.

Many episodes follow, in which the man, who insists on pursuing her, is about to discover her true profession. For example, he invites her to an oyster bar where, after having drunk several bottles of beer, she does things she can't remember, and is later haunted by the fear that during her mental lapse she may have said, "What the hell, I'm a whore!" Or else, the man comes to the México Lindo with his teammates and she has to hide under a table, and so forth.

The story ends on the night the Whoremaster comes to the cabaret and finds Blanca downcast, asks her why, and she tells him that the soccer player is dead. She then launches into a description, with a wealth of realistic detail, of a bloody highway smashup. Blanca never mentioned the soccer player again after that night and the Whoremaster could not bring himself to ask about him.

4

Her illness:

In September, 1962—when the Plan de Abajo brothels were closed and all the girls were living and working at the México Lindo—Blanca discovered that she was pregnant. It was not the first time. As on previous occasions, she went to the Skeleton for help, who—according to her own statement—prepared an infusion of rue and wormwood leaves, which the patient drank hot, one cupful three times a day. This remedy, prepared many times before by the Skeleton and used with excellent results by the women who worked for the Baladro sisters, was considered infallible for inducing an abortion. Blanca took it for two months without effect, in view of which she decided to consult the Baladros. Serafina advised an operation and told her that she and her sister would pay for it.

Dr. Arellano, whose signature appeared on a number of IOUs held by Arcángela, admits that he performed the operation in exchange for these IOUs after considerable urging by the sisters in the face of his warning that it was dangerous because of the advanced stage of the pregnancy. He operated on Blanca one day in November, with the Skeleton assisting. The operation was not completely successful, because the patient hemorrhaged profusely, which the doctor attributed to a hematological imbalance produced by the large quantity of rue and wormwood she had taken. He had to give her eight vitamin K injections before the bleeding finally stopped at eleven o'clock that night and everybody thought Blanca was saved. The doctor left the house after Arcángela turned the IOUs over to him. Serafina and Arcángela went down to attend to the cabaret and the Skeleton to supervise the rooms. The patient remained in her room, asleep. The next morning when the Skeleton opened the door and went in, carrying a glass of orange juice, she noted that Blanca's features looked twisted. On closer inspection it was apparent that the entire left side of her body was paralyzed.

Dr. Arellano refused to visit the patient. As a consequence, Serafina called in Dr. Abdulio Meneses, over the objections of Arcángela who was fearful of the cost and possible complications. He examined Blanca and after asking a number of bumbling questions with respect to how the illness started—which must have received even clumsier answers—decided that she should be moved to his private hospital for intensive treatment.

Blanca was admitted on December 4, 1962 to the Sacred Heart Sanatorium, which had the reputation of being the best in the region. Serafina Baladro's name appears on the admission record as Blanca's closest relative and the person responsible for all bills. Several of the girls came to visit her on the fifth and the sixth and found her much improved; the Whoremaster brought her a bunch of red roses on the seventh and was unable —according to one of the nurses who was present—to control a grimace of horror at seeing her so deformed. Humberto was murdered on the eighth; the México Lindo was shut down on the tenth; and on the eleventh, Dr. Meneses, having decided that Blanca's bill would never be paid, ordered treatment to be suspended and the patient discharged.

The record of her discharge from the Sacred Heart Sanatorium gives the impression that the patient was picked up by relatives. (There is an illegible signature on the slip.) That same day, Blanca was admitted to the San Pedro de las Corrientes Municipal Hospital under the name of María Méndez—the only one she ever bore in her life that she herself had not invented—with no indication on the admittance slip of next of kin or attending physician.

The Whoremaster went to visit Blanca in January and the receptionist at the Sacred Heart Sanatorium informed him that the patient had been discharged and picked up by relatives. The Whoremaster assumed that Blanca must have recovered and was back with the Baladros, and so did not look for her any further. He felt certain that the sisters would soon reappear in a new place, either in San Pedro or some other town in the region and that, being one of their steadiest customers, he would be notified whenever that happened.

The Baladros, however, in their distress over the death of Humberto, the closing down of the México Lindo, and the tumult of moving, forgot about Blanca for a time. When they finally remembered her, they took it for granted that she was still at the Sacred Heart Sanatorium—with a huge bill piled up that Serafina had assumed the responsibility for paying. This was the reason they made no attempt to visit her or to check up on how she was doing.

Finally, in March, the Whoremaster had to make a

trip to Concepción to collect a bill. (He is an automobile salesman.) After taking care of his business, in an upsurge of erotic nostalgia he decided to have a look at the outside of the Casino del Danzón. He left his car near the square, walked to Independence Street, and was standing before the sealed door when, to his surprise, the Skeleton, on her way to buy lard, came out of the adjoining house. They embraced like the old friends they were and the Skeleton told him two lies—that she was coming from a visit to an old acquaintance of hers, señora Benavides, and that the other girls were all living in Muérdago. When the Whoremaster asked about Blanca, she told him that she was at the Sacred Heart Sanatorium.

That is how it came out that Blanca had disappeared. As they were strolling together toward the butcher shop, the Whoremaster got the idea of notifying the police. The Skeleton begged him not to, and in explaining why it was necessary to be so discreet, she was compelled to tell him where the Baladros, she, and the other women were living. The Whoremaster agreed to hunt for Blanca on his own and if he found her to leave word by telephone at the taxi stand where Ladder worked.

Three days after this conversation, the Whoremaster found Blanca in the first place he looked—the women's ward of the municipal hospital. She did not even remotely resemble the woman he knew. Her mental faculties were impaired and her face so grotesquely distorted that it cost him an effort to believe it was she. The invalid's speech was practically unintelligible because one side of her mouth was paralyzed.

The Whoremaster was so upset by the experience that after notifying the Skeleton, as he had promised, he wanted to know nothing more of Blanca.

5

The Skeleton visited Blanca the next day. When the hospital superintendent noticed that the patient María Méndez had a visitor, he called the Skeleton aside, informed her that the woman's condition was hopeless, and asked her to notify her relatives to come and take her away because other patients who could be helped were waiting for a bed.

6

The day after that, the Baladros arrived at the municipal hospital in Ladder's car, signed the necessary papers, and took Blanca to the Casino del Danzón with them.

According to the statements of witnesses, two of the women carried Blanca down from the room in the mornings to the yard, where they would leave her to bask in the sun curled up in a galvanized metal bathtub. Later on, they would carry her back up to her room. She was completely emaciated, her only food the gruels that the Skeleton prepared for her, and she gave no sign of understanding when she was spoken to and nobody understood what she said.

In May, Arcángela—who was constantly complaining of how much it was costing her to feed all those mouths while nothing was coming in—decided that inasmuch as Blanca was unable to chew anyway, it would be just as well to remove her gold teeth and sell them to compensate in part for all the trouble she was causing. Arcángela entered Blanca's room one morning with that intention and tried to pull out the teeth, but the invalid clamped her jaws shut so tightly that after a brief struggle she gave up the attempt.

On July 5, the Skeleton took a trip to Pedrones to consult a famous healer, Tomasa X, on how to cure paralysis. It was Tomasa X who explained the treatment that is described below and which she recommended as being very effective. Back in Concepción, the Skeleton asked permission from her employers to attempt a cure and it was granted.

(Several days went by when the Skeleton and various of the other women were busy preparing the *mole* that was to be the main dish at the celebration of the blessing of the farm.)

The day of July 17 comes. Ticho wires the legs of three tables together to make them firm and places them in the middle of the cabaret, chosen by the Skeleton as the most appropriate place for applying the treatment. Having done this, Ticho leaves the house, having no idea what was to take place later on. At eleven o'clock, fires are kindled in two braziers which are set on either side of the tables. Marta, Rosa, Evelia, and Feliza, acting as the Skeleton's assistants, place six flatirons to heat on the braziers. The Skeleton rubs the invalid's body with a tincture of the bark of the *cazaguate* tree. The assistants tie the patient to the tables with two sheets. The Baladro sisters watch the treatment from the balcony of the cabaret. The assistants cover the patient's body with a light flannel blanket. Marta, a pitcher of water in her hand, is in charge of wetting the blanket to which the Skeleton applies the hot irons; Rosa changes the irons as they cool off; Evelia and Feliza hold the patient down when she writhes.

The prescription is the following: Apply hot irons to the dampened blanket on the patient's paralyzed side until the blanket turns dark brown.

In the beginning, it seemed as though the treatment was working. Not only were the invalid's screams more coherent than her speech had been in the last few months, but it was also noted that when the irons were applied, she moved muscles that had been inert for a long time. Afterward, the invalid fainted. The women tried to bring her around by giving her Coca-Cola to drink, but it was impossible to make her swallow it, the liquid dribbling out between her lips. The Skeleton hesitated momentarily about whether or not the treatment should be continued. She decided to go on with it and kept applying the irons until the blanket turned dark brown as specified by señora Tomasa. They tried giving her Coca-Cola again, but without success. On lifting the blanket off the patient's body they were surprised to see that her skin was stuck to the cloth.

"Cover her up! Cover her up!" Serafina screamed from the balcony, they say.

One of the women ran for another blanket. The others

untied the invalid. After covering her, they carried her to her room and put her to bed. She did not regain consciousness. The girls and the Baladros stayed with her until midnight, the hour at which she stopped breathing.

XI
Various Views

1

María del Carmen Regulez states in regard to that day, that after breakfast the Skeleton told her and three of the other girls: "Go out for a walk. Take your time, stop in at the market, stay awhile and look over the vegetables. Don't come back before five o'clock." She gave each of them one peso for food.

These orders surprised the girls, but they obeyed. As they were walking along Cuauhtemoc Street they went by a garage where three boys who knew them worked. On seeing them pass, the boys followed behind, "making vulgar remarks." They kept on walking to the edge of town and then headed toward the reservoir where the boys caught up with them and "took advantage of them" behind some bushes. After having a bite to eat in the market, they walked around the square until it got to be five o'clock.

When they returned to the Casino del Danzón, they went to the kitchen with the idea of notifying the Skeleton that they were back. There was no one there nor any signs of food, the fire had not been made, and there was no charcoal on the grates.

María del Carmen went out to the yard to take in the clothes she had hung on the line. She noticed that Blanca's tub was not under the lemon tree, but next to the cabaret door, which was closed.

When she returned to the kitchen she found several

of the other girls who had also just gotten back. Eleven
women went out that day—something that rarely
happened.

She says that when she got upstairs she heard voices
in Blanca's room and was very curious but did not dare
go in because she thought she recognized the voices of
the Baladros among them; that she stayed in her room
for a while and then, on hearing a noise in the hall,
opened the door a crack and saw Arcángela and the
Skeleton walking toward the stairs; that she heard Arcángela say, "It was all your fault!"

There was nothing but orange-leaf tea for supper that
night. Several of the girls asked Feliza what had happened, but she would not say. The rumor began to circu-
late that Blanca had taken a turn for the worse. When
she went up to her room—María del Carmen says—she
noticed that the tub was no longer by the cabaret door.

She says that she slept for a while but was awakened
by hunger pangs. She heard voices and footsteps and
she intended to get up to see what was happening, but
fell asleep again.

María del Carmen woke up early the next morning—
she was hungry—and went down to the kitchen. The
Skeleton had lit the fire and was fixing cracklings in
green tomato sauce for Ticho's breakfast. María del
Carmen asked if Blanca was any worse and the Skeleton
answered, "She got so bad we had to take her to the hospital again."

María del Carmen says that for several days she believed that what the Skeleton had told her was true.

2

Ticho states with reference to the events that took place
that night and the day before, that, after tying the legs
of the tables together and putting them where the Skeleton told him, he asked for permission to go to work.
(After the México Lindo was closed, the Baladros
stopped Ticho's salary and he had to take odd jobs load-
ing and unloading trucks and carrying goods.)

He relates that he went to the Barajas Brothers'

warehouse and was shifting crates of tomatoes, baskets of chili peppers, and sacks of potatoes from leaky rooms to dry ones, that he knocked off at two o'clock and went across the street to the market for a giblets taco, that he returned to the warehouse and continued working until eight o'clock at night when the boss called a halt and paid him the twenty pesos he had been promised.

He states that when he returned to the Casino del Danzón there was nobody around to notify that he was back—that is to say, neither the Baladros nor the Skeleton—that he went into the kitchen, saw that there was no dinner, and then went to the charcoal bin in which he lived. He lay down on the cot and fell asleep.

He states: I couldn't say what time it was when I woke up. The Skeleton was at the door of the bin holding an oil lamp. I said, "My little Skeleton," and I started to lift her skirt. But she didn't want to. She just said, "Come with me," and left. I thought she was going to give me some dinner and so I followed her, but instead of going into the kitchen she went out to the yard where she stopped and said to me, "Get a pick and shovel out of the shed."

When I came back with the tools, the Skeleton walked off and I followed. We got as far as the other end of the yard—the northwest corner—where she put the lamp down on the ground and said to me, "I want you to do a job without making any noise."

(She ordered him to dig a rectangular hole two paces long by one pace wide and deep enough so that when he stood up in it his armpits would be on a level with the ground. After giving these directions, the Skeleton went back to the house. Ticho dug easily in the soft earth until his pick began hitting stones and Arcángela and the Skeleton came out of the house and told him to stop. The hole was hardly a meter deep. Ticho goes on to say: Señora Arcángela said, "Leave it at that. It's better than to risk waking the neighbors.")

The Skeleton took me to the kitchen, made me a fried egg, and gave me a mug of orange-leaf tea with a shot of alcohol in it. I said, "My little Skeleton" again and she didn't want to again so I went back to the bin and went to sleep.

It was getting light when I woke up. The Skeleton was

96

at the door of the bin with the lamp. I said, "My little Skeleton," but she pushed my hand away and again said, "Come with me."

We went to the other end of the yard. I saw that somebody had shoveled earth into the hole I made, filling it about half full. "I want you to finish filling this hole," the Skeleton told me, "and to tamp it down good with the mesquite stump. And, now—get this—if there is any dirt left over, I want you to spread it around the yard with the shovel so that nobody will notice that there was ever a hole there."

I did the job just like I was ordered. By the time the Skeleton saw the hole filled, the earth tamped down, and the leftover spread around the yard, it was broad daylight. She took me to the kitchen and gave me a plate of cracklings she had just prepared for breakfast. While I was eating them, one of the girls came into the kitchen and asked the Skeleton how Blanca was doing. The Skeleton answered that she took so sick that they had to send her to the hospital again. That was when I got the idea of what it was I had been doing all night.

3

Captain Bedoya states:

July the seventeenth sticks in my mind because it was a very hectic day. Major Marín, who brought the payroll, arrived two days late at the same time as the hay truck that was supposed to have been there by the fourteenth. (He explains that the unloading was delayed because, according to regulations, the detachment had to line up and stand inspection before receiving their pay.) I left the camp with barely enough time to rush to the telegraph office before the money-order window closed. (Captain Bedoya bought a fifty-peso draft to the order of Carmelita Bedoya—his little daughter—accompanied by a message that read: "Congratulations from daddy on the occasion of your saint's day." It was sent to an address in Mexico City. The captain's wife was also named Carmen, but he sent no message or remembrance to her. It should be noted that although the captain had money in the bank he preferred to wait until Major Marín arrived with his pay to send his daughter her present, even if it meant she would get it a day late.) From the telegraph office—Captain Bedoya continues—I went to Serafina's.

I found her in the dining room, upset and trembling. I asked what was wrong and she told me that she had had a nerve-wracking day because Blanca took a very bad turn. She looked so jittery that I said good night to her, had some supper at the Gómez Hotel, and spent the night on the post. The following day, Serafina told me they had to take Blanca to the hospital.

I said, "The municipal hospital, I hope."

She answered that, as a matter of fact, the municipal hospital was exactly where they had taken her.

Captain Bedoya had always considered it insanity for the Baladros to be spending money on Blanca. When they hospitalized her in Dr. Meneses's sanatorium, several witnesses heard him make the following comment: "It's throwing away money. Maybe that woman will be able to walk again some day but nobody is ever going to fix that face of hers and what good is a whore that gives you the horrors to look at?"

When Blanca was finally brought back to the Casino del Danzón from the hospital, Serafina preferred to say nothing to the captain, until one day he went out to the yard and found the paralyzed woman lying in the bathtub under the lemon tree.

"What's this?" they say he asked several of the women who were nearby.

They told him it was Blanca. The captain then said, "That woman is no good anymore. What they ought to do is have Ticho carry her out to the garbage dump one of these nights and leave her there for the dogs to eat."

(Possibly because of such remarks, Serafina preferred not to tell him what had really happened to Blanca.)

Captain Bedoya says: One night in the beginning of August when we were in bed together and the light was out, Serafina told me that she was losing hope of ever being able to reopen the business. I was glad that she was finally seeing reason, because I had given up on

98

that a long time ago. It did not occur to me, though, to ask her what made her change her mind.

I woke up in a good mood the next morning, put on my underwear shorts and a *guayabera* shirt, and went out to the back of the house to breathe in some fresh morning air. It was a day without clouds, like in the dry season. As I was looking up at the sky I saw vultures. There were two of them and they were flying in circles around a spot that seemed to be right over my head.

I swear I am an atheist, but I got such an awful feeling I crossed myself.

4

Extract of the confrontation between Aurora Bautista and Eustiquio Natera—known as Ticho—during the investigation:

Aurora Bautista: "Isn't it the truth that when you were carrying a sack of charcoal into the house one day, Doña Arcángela said to you, 'Cut off a *cazaguate* branch and drive off those goddam birds that are walking around in the yard.' Isn't it true she said that to you?"

Ticho: "I do not recall that occasion."

Aurora Bautista: "And don't you remember that you chopped off a handful of branches from the bush and that you went over to where the vultures were and scared them off and that they flew around for a while and then landed back on the ground in the same place again?"

Ticho: "I have chased off vultures more than once in my life. Which time is it you want me to remember?"

Aurora Bautista: "The time that doña Serafina couldn't stand it anymore, went for her pistol, gave it to you, and said, 'Shoot the damn things!' And then doña Arcángela came out to the back and said to you, 'What are you people trying to do, scare the neighbors?' Do you remember, now?"

Ticho: "It must have been somebody else who was there at the time."

Aurora Bautista: "And I suppose you weren't the one either who was in the kitchen with the Skeleton, Luz

María, and me when Captain Bedoya came in and asked for a glass of water and then after he drank it he said, 'I wonder where that stink could be coming from.' And the Skeleton said, 'It must be that dead dog next door.' Weren't you the one who was sitting there then eating a tortilla? (Ticho gave evasive answers to this question and the following ones Aurora Bautista put to him.)

"Isn't it true that you came in one day with a can and doña Arcángela asked you how much the gasoline cost? Don't you remember the night you took the pick and shovel and dug a hole in the rear of the yard? . . . and later that night you made a fire that burned for a long time and the next morning the air smelled foul?"

Ticho: "I think you must have dreamed what you are saying. It never happened."

XII
The Fourteenth
of September

1

On September 14, the Baladro sisters had a meeting with señor Sirenio Pantoja—proprietor of houses of prostitution in Jaloste—for the purpose of negotiating the sale of their remaining fifteen girls. This decision suggests that they had by then given up all hope of reopening their businesses.

The meeting took place at eleven o'clock in the morning in Pedrones at an ice cream parlor by the name of La Siberia. The Baladros were obsessed with keeping don Sirenio from suspecting that they were living in the Casino del Danzón—the previous deal with the same man for the eleven women had been arranged on a bench in the Pedrones square—without taking into account, probably, that this secret was known to the women they were selling to him.

It seems that don Sirenio was looking for better terms—the situation was not the same as on the first occasion when he had sought them out; this time, the sisters were making him the proposition. Maintaining that he had had heavy expenses recently, he offered three hundred pesos per girl. This offer was rejected by the Baladros who acted as though they were about to leave in a huff. Don Sirenio went up to four hundred. The Baladros remained in the ice cream parlor. When don Sirenio offered six hundred, they closed the deal. The result of their having spent the morning there will be seen later.

2

The balcony in the cabaret of the Casino del Danzón was not part of the architect's original plan; it broke the illusion of being at the bottom of the sea that the rest of the decor sought to create, and provoked impassioned protests, it is said, from the young decorator who had acted as adviser to the Baladros on the construction of the brothel. The balcony is there, nevertheless.

It was Serafina's idea. On her visit to Acapulco, she saw from the street—and never forgot—a vocal trio singing on a balcony, accompanying themselves on guitars, while the tourists ate in the patio below. It occurred to her that on a gala night—that is to say, when a politician or some influential person came in with friends and wanted the place closed to the public—it would be nice to hire a trio, and when the people down on the dance floor and at the tables least expected it, to have the balcony doors open and the singers come out singing "Las Mañanitas" in honor of whoever was paying the bill.

The balcony was built, but no singers ever made use of it. Arcángela and *licenciado* Canales appeared on it the night of the inauguration of the Casino del Danzón when he gave the "Cry of Independence" that cost him his job, it was from there Arcángela and Serafina watched Blanca's treatment, and it also played its part in what is now to follow.

It should be noted that the railing of this balcony was never properly installed. The ironworker who made it warned the contractor that it was not secure; the contractor, after checking and finding that this was in fact the case, ordered a mason to reinforce it; the mason promised to take care of it, but never did.

Months later, after the building was finished, Arcángela said, "That railing is loose and has to be fixed. If anybody ever leans on it good and hard, it could break

102

off and he'll land head first on the floor—and that floor is four meters down."

Following this observation, nobody thought about the railing again until the fourteenth of September.

3

To get to the balcony one goes down the hall that leads to the rooms. The women were in the hall when the fight started.

This is more or less the picture: There are two women locked in struggle, their faces very close, gripping each other's hair with both hands. Their features are distorted, eyes now screwed tight with pain, now bulging in their sockets, mouths twisted, lips flecked with spittle; their dresses are disarranged and torn, shreds of a brassiere showing through a bodice. They move together, bodies very close, as though dancing—three steps in one direction, two in another, from time to time, a foot stamped on, a kick in the shin, a knee in the groin. The noises that come from the women are animallike—grunts, gasps, snorts, an occasional short ugly word: "whore," "bitch," and so on.

The women were alone when the fight began, but it went on for so long that the others in the house realized that something special was happening and had come out of their rooms into the hall to watch. (The Skeleton was at the market.)

Thirteen women look on while the two tear each other's hair out without anyone trying to stop them. The reason is that the two women fighting are "soul mates" —that is, lovers—and the others consider their fight a personal matter in which the community should not interfere. And so, the women followed the bitter and even struggle—a shove one way, a pull the other—closely but silently, thinking that it would stop when the combatants were exhausted. The fight would have ended without blood being shed if the Baladros, who were getting out of Ladder's car, had moved a bit faster; they would have been in time to yell and break it up. Or if the fighters had not had the bad luck to reach the balcony just as one gave the other a violent push that made her hit the railing with her buttock, breaking it loose and causing the two of them, still clutching each other by the hair, to plunge to the floor. Their skulls hit the cement and broke like eggs. The lives of both came to an end at the same moment. Their names were Evelia and Feliza.

4

The Baladros came in by way of señora Benavides's house, passed through the opening between the two buildings, and were crossing their dining room when they heard steps, thuds, gasps. Arcángela was about to shout, "What's going on?" when she heard, first a resonant sound (buttock against railing), followed by a rending noise (the railing breaking loose), a reverberating crash (the railing hitting the floor), and a sharp crack (heads against concrete).

It is possible that some of those who saw the accident may have screamed, that one or several of the women rushed down the stairs, but death always ends by imposing silence on those who contemplate it.

One may assume, then, that when the Baladros came through the door that leads from the house into the cabaret, there was silence. They entered a room filled with plaster dust, distinguishing first the twisted railing, then the bodies and, finally, on looking up, the four, five, six, or more women in the frame of the railing-less balcony, staring down.

The suspicions may be ignored—"Who pushed them?"—as well as the recriminations: "You are to blame for not having separated them!" and so forth. The Baladros must have finally come to the realization that the accident was entirely the victims' fault. Also, they discovered on one of the bodies the possible motive for the quarrel: Blanca's gold teeth.

Evelia had Blanca's gold teeth in her brassiere, it being the only part of her clothing in which anything could be hidden since she wore one-piece décolleté dresses without sleeves or pockets.

The story of Blanca's gold teeth is as follows: Arcángela tried to pull them out of their owner's jaws while she was ill, but was unable to do so; when Blanca died, Arcángela had so many things on her mind that she forgot to remove them from the corpse; however, when it became necessary to disinter and burn it, she remembered the teeth and decided to salvage them. It was then that she discovered they were gone.

She said nothing, but brooded about the matter for weeks; Blanca's teeth had been stolen by one of the women living in the house. Serafina, Ticho, and the Skeleton were above suspicion—at least, Arcángela liked to think so—consequently, the thief had to be one of the four women who were involved in the treatment and then the burial. On reaching this point in her reasoning, Arcángela's mind would cloud and she was unable to get any further toward unraveling the mystery. Not only was the guilty one taking refuge under her roof—a roof she and her sister had built with their money—but she was eating the tortillas they were paying for. And, on top of that, she had stolen the gold teeth that were rightfully theirs in return for the sacrifices—and enormous expense—involved in the course of Blanca's illness.

The mystery was cleared up on September 14. The gold teeth were sticking halfway out of Evelia's brassiere. Arcángela saw them when she bent over the body, took them, put them in her pocket, and sold them two weeks later to a jeweler in Pedrones for five hundred pesos.

Not only did the guilty one give up the stolen property to its rightful owner when she was found out, but she had already received her punishment.

5

This sudden turn of events leaves part of the story indeterminable. It is only possible to surmise. Evelia and Feliza's relationship was of ten years' standing, their companions say. They were constant and placid lovers held up as examples and even envied by other employees. According to the reports, although they lived as husband and wife—Feliza served Evelia at the table and mended her clothes; Evelia administered Feliza's earnings—they discharged their duties in the brothel conscientiously. After ten years of living together in absolute harmony, with never any sign of discord between them—the slip that Feliza had washed for Evelia was hanging on the clothes line—they ended by killing each other.

The explanation for what happened should perhaps be sought in Blanca's gold teeth.

Years before, when Blanca thought up the show in which three women had to take part, she chose Evelia and Feliza as her co-performers. It appears that a relationship was established between the three that went beyond the show. Evelia and Feliza visited Blanca at Dr. Meneses's sanatorium, helped Ladder get her into the car after Serafina signed the papers releasing Blanca from the San Pedro de las Corrientes Municipal Hospital, and were the ones who carried Blanca down from her room every morning, put her in the galvanized tub under the lemon tree, and carried her up again in the afternoons. They wanted to take part in Blanca's treatment—it was Feliza who tried to revive her with Coca-Cola and Evelia who ran for the blanket.

Hypothesis: One of the two, either Evelia or Feliza, removed the teeth from the corpse during a lapse when she was left alone with it, said nothing to anybody, and the other one discovered them in her friend's possession three months later, considered the theft and the secrecy an act of treachery, and grabbed her by the hair.

Another hypothesis: Blanca, feeling so very ill and knowing that Arcángela would pull her teeth out, preferred to give them away while she was still alive to her favorite—either Evelia or Feliza—and when the other discovered that she was not the favored one she was seized by a fit of jealousy, with the consequences that have been seen.

It could have been like that.

It is necessary, now, to return to the moment when Arcángela and Serafina entered the cabaret and saw the bodies, the twisted railing, the gold teeth, and so forth, in a cloud of plaster dust, looked up and saw five, six, seven . . . up to thirteen women's faces peering down from the balcony frame.

At that moment, without any of the people concerned realizing it, the relationship between the proprietresses of the house and their employees underwent a radical change. Those staring down from the balcony were witnesses to the presence of two corpses below and, later, to the way in which they were disposed of. The Baladros run the house, are the leaders of this community, and consequently responsible for what happens in it.

Apparently, everything becomes simplified. For example, now it is unnecessary to dig the grave in the middle of the night or try to be quiet so as not to awaken the girls. At six o'clock in the evening when Ticho returned from a job—carrying bags of cement—the Skeleton led him to the corner of the yard where Blanca was buried and ordered him to dig another pit a few meters away double the width of the first and one meter, eighty centimeters deep and not to worry about the noise made by the pick and crowbar against the hardpan and stones. Ticho obeyed and at twelve o'clock the same night Evelia and Feliza were buried.

Captain Bedoya did not come to see Serafina that night because of duties on the post, nor the next night since it was the eve of the Independence Day parade and the troops were confined to quarters. On the evening of the sixteenth, the captain arrived at the house, mortified: Just as the parade turned into Avenue Juárez in Pedrones, his dapple-gray horse reared and he was nearly thrown. To make matters worse, his saber fell to the ground and a little boy picked it up and returned it to him, humiliating him even more. He felt that he had made a fool of himself before his men and hundreds of onlookers.

As he walked, downcast, hands in pockets, toward Independence Street, the captain had said to himself, All I want to do is drink until I forget my shame.

That was his mood when Serafina gave him the news that Evelia and Feliza had died and were buried in the backyard. (Serafina, who had never told Bedoya about what happened to Blanca, reproached herself when she heard him asking, in his ignorance, what it was that smelled dead.) Serafina opened the conversation by saying, "I am going to tell you something, because there shouldn't be any secrets between us," and so forth.

When the news was broken, the captain commented, "That's just fine! Now, all you need is for the rest of the thirteen to die so you can bury the whole crew in the yard."

Months later, during the trial, the captain explained that this remark was intended as a joke, but the judge did not believe him.

On September 18, Serafina telephoned don Sirenio Pantoja to say that she "deeply regretted" having to tell him that her sister had changed her mind and decided not to sell him the girls as they had agreed. Don Sirenio says that from the tone of Serafina's voice he could tell that there would have been no point in his offering to raise the price. He thought that either they had sold them to another customer or decided not to sell at all.

XIII
Martial Law

1

Every year on the twenty-fourth of September, one of the girls, María del Carmen Régulez, visited her mother, whose name was Mercedes.

Every year, two evenings before that date, María del Carmen would ask Serafina for permission to be absent from work on the night of the twenty-fourth, and Arcángela for money either out of her account or, if the balance was low, as an advance. María del Carmen states that she had never had any problems on that score before. She had always gotten permission from Serafina and the money from Arcángela. On the twenty-third, María del Carmen would go to the market where she would buy a bunch of flowers—gladiolas, preferably—which were always withered by the time they reached her mother's outstretched arms, a length of dress goods, a shawl, or a pair of shoes. The trip started at dawn the following day because María del Carmen had to change buses three times to reach the *rancho* where her family lived. She would get off the third bus at a point halfway up a bleak hill and walk along a barely distinguishable footpath until she came to a *pitahaya* tree. The houses and the cactus patch of the settlement could be seen from there.

The dogs would forget María del Carmen from one year to the next and every year her mother and sisters-in-law would come out of the kitchen to quiet them;

every year, on finding themselves together again, the women would cry; every year they would go into the kitchen, sit around the brazier, and talk—someone had died, a baby had been born, the crops had been lost. The men would return from the fields in midafternoon, the family would sit down at the table, María del Carmen helped wait on them. Only her mother knew about her daughter's profession—she was the one who had sold her. The rest of the family thought she was a servant. At night they would drink orange-leaf tea spiked with alcohol and get drunk. The next day at dawn, María del Carmen started back to the whorehouse.

On September 22 of that year, María del Carmen asked Serafina for permission to go to the *rancho* and, for the first time, it was refused.

"My sister has decided," she told her, "that nobody can go out except the girls the Skeleton takes with her to bring the food from the market."

She did not explain the reason for this prohibition, nor did she tell her how long it would last. María del Carmen did not dare ask questions on either point because like all the Baladros' employees she was afraid of them. She did, however, tell the other women that Serafina had forbidden her to go to the *rancho* and that only the girls who went to market with the Skeleton—they were always the same two—could leave the house. These conversations repeated over and over again in the lethargic atmosphere of the inactive brothel, made the eleven women, denied the privilege of going out, feel as though they were prisoners and, what is more significant, united.

2

Rosa X and Marta X were the two girls who went out with the Skeleton to buy the food.

Rosa's name appears in the San Pedro de las Corrientes Antivenereal Disease Register, successively, as Margarita Rosa, Rosa de las Nieves, and Maria del Rosal. At the whorehouse she was called just Rosa. She had a reputation for being meek and servile. When the

110

whorehouse opened in the evening—those who worked with her say—she was always the first girl down from her room to pass inspection by the madam—either Serafina or Arcángela, she worked for them both. If any fault was found—flaking nail polish or a hair bow that did not go with the color of her dress—Rosa would return to her room without grumbling—something no other girl did—and try to correct it. In the closed-down whorehouse, it was known that Rosa could be counted on to do the hardest and most disagreeable or unnecessary jobs, such as cleaning the caked surfaces of greasy pots or carrying the heaviest basket from the market.

She also had the reputation of being two-faced and an informer. This reputation had its basis in two incidents. On one occasion, a drunken customer took his wristwatch off and left it on the table, and one of the women who had been sitting with him picked it up and hid it away. Rosa was the only person who saw her do this. Arcángela intervened and before the evening was over compelled the girl to return the watch and slapped a fine on her that took her months to pay off. On another occasion, Carmelo X, a waiter in the Molino Street house, worked out a system for cheating Serafina which consisted of giving out tokens for fictitious drinks to various of the girls who were in with him; they handed in the tokens to Serafina, collected their commissions and split with Carmelo. This lasted until he made the mistake of inviting Rosa into his organization. The next day he was fired.

Aside from being servile and two-faced, Rosa had no other virtues. Her complexion was sallow and she suffered from a permanent cold—the Skeleton said that every time she blew her nose it sounded like a bugle call —and wore an expression of martyrdom. Any man who approached her was either very drunk or unable to see clearly in the dim light of the cabaret. Those who knew her say that her favorite topic of conversation at the tables was her bad luck—"life gave me a raw deal" being one of her frequent remarks. Not many customers ventured to go up to Rosa's room and even fewer did so a second time.

The Baladros put up with Rosa for ten and a half years, partly because of her servility and partly because she was an informer, but mainly because they were unable to get rid of her. First, they passed her from one to the other, then, they tried several times to sell her, but after seeing her, any potential purchaser would back out. Finally, the Baladros gave up and used her to get rid of troublesome or insolvent customers.

Rosa's earnings were meager and she piled up the biggest debt that appears in Arcángela's book over the ten years—45,400 pesos. It is possible that Arcángela, with the illogicalness characteristic of greed, nourished the illusion that Rosa might suddenly become attractive and one day begin to pay off all the money she owed the family.

3

It was Rosa's misfortune that she walked through the hall between the rooms at an hour when she should not have.

On learning from María del Carmen that nobody was going to be allowed out except the two who accompanied the Skeleton, one of the girls, Aurora Bautista, decided to escape from the whorehouse.

She mentioned the idea to three of the other girls and they agreed to go along with her. They met several times in the room of one of them to make plans. It was decided that the break should be made at night, between eleven o'clock, when everybody was asleep, and midnight, when the last bus to Pedrones left. As far as getting out of the house was concerned, it was impossible to use the same route as the Baladros because the key to the dining room would be needed and it hung in Serafina's bosom; to climb over one of the walls meant landing in a strange yard amidst unfriendly dogs; the only solution, then, was to use a ladder to reach the roof of the Casino and to jump across to the roof of señora Benavides's house, from where they could easily get down to the street level and leave through the front gate, which was bolted on the inside. The house had a ladder that was kept in the shed where Ticho slept. Ticho was known for sleeping like the dead.

On the afternoon the four women were deciding to make their escape from the whorehouse by means of the ladder, they heard a noise in the hall as though somebody might be eavesdropping, and fell silent. Luz María, whose room it was, got up and cautiously opened the door. Nobody was directly outside it, but Rosa was several meters away walking down the hall toward her . . .

For a while, the women weighed the possibility that Rosa had overheard, but reached the conclusion that it was unlikely. However, to be on the safe side, it was decided not to delay and to make the move that same night.

One can imagine their baggage—the string bags, the cartons tied up with rope, and so forth; each made a selection of her prized possessions—the orange-colored evening dress, the patent-leather slippers—taking into consideration the jump that had to be made and the possibility that it might be necessary to run through the streets. They say that they scraped together enough among the four of them to cover the fare to Pedrones plus forty-five pesos extra, which they planned to use to keep on traveling as far away as possible in any direction from Concepción.

At night, when everything was quiet, the women, barefooted, met in the hall, went downstairs, and across the patio. One of them, Luz María, confesses that she picked up a round stone so big she had to carry it in both arms to drop on Ticho's head in case he woke up. They went into the shed, which had no door. Ticho did not wake up, but the women, feeling around in the dark, realized that the ladder was not there.

They came out of the shed dismayed and met in the kitchen in the dark, where they held a whispered conference and reached the conclusion that Rosa had squealed on them. They became infuriated.

The subsequent scene must have been as follows: A woman is asleep in a large bed in a dark room; the door opens silently—the Baladros had all bolts removed from the rooms after the whorehouse was closed so that the girls could not lock themselves in; silhouettes cross the threshold against the penumbra; the door closes.

It is not known if Rosa woke up when the others turned on the light, when they pulled the covers back, or

113

when they began to beat her. Nor is it known if the beating took place in the dark or with the light on. Nor if Rosa was struck dumb with fear, if the attackers prevented her from crying out, or if she shouted at the top of her lungs without anybody hearing.

"They gave her the shoe treatment," says the Skeleton in describing this revenge.

Rosa's wounds were produced by the high heels of the shoes with which the girls beat her.

The following day, when all the women were having breakfast in the kitchen and Rosa did not appear, the Skeleton went up to her room to see if anything was wrong with her. She heard a groan as she approached the door of her room. Rosa was in bed, semiconscious, a blanket over her. There were no marks on her face, but her body, particularly the buttocks, was covered with black-and-blue welts and wounds which later became infected and developed into running sores because of lack of attention.

4

Rosa did not know, or did not want to say, who attacked her. The Baladros had made up their minds to punish this "disorderly conduct" severely, but did not know to whom to attribute it—which indicates that Rosa had not divulged the escape plan and that the ladder was missing from its usual place only by chance—and could think of no way of finding out who the culprits were.

The woman who served the madams their dinner that afternoon asserts that Captain Bedoya was the one who advised them how to figure out who had been involved.

The woman saw him walking around the yard, his head down, stooping every little while to pick up a stone, weighing it in his hand, and making a pile of those that were spherical and neither very light nor very heavy. Then he went around examining the floors of the house until he found one that seemed most appropriate for the purpose he had in mind. It was a small patio next to the kitchen which was part of the original construction and paved with broken stone embedded in concrete.

The Baladros called the women together in this place and Arcángela said to them, "Who beat up Rosa?"

There was no answer.

Arcángela ordered the women to kneel on the irregular surface and when they had obeyed, the captain, who was present from the beginning, ordered them to hold their arms stretched out at their sides, shoulder-high, palms up. When they were all in that position, the captain and the Skeleton took stones from the pile he had gotten together and put one in each hand.

When a woman dropped a stone Arcángela struck her with a stick. (This was the first instance of corporal punishment in the history of the Casino del Danzón.) This stick and several others had been cut off the *cazaguate* bush by the captain that same afternoon. They say that the guilty ones confessed in less than fifteen minutes, upon which punishment of the others was suspended.

The Skeleton brought Aurora Bautista, Luz María, María del Carmen, and Socorro into the Baghdad Salon where they were subjected to another punishment, also devised by the captain. It consisted of each in turn beating the other three until all four were so bruised that they were unable to move for days after.

Over the twenty-three years that Captain Bedoya served in the army there is no record of his having administered or ordered the administration of any corporal punishment nor does any soldier who served with or under him recall his ever having been involved in any act of cruelty. When questioned during the trial with respect to his participation in the "penitence" and the blows the women gave one another, the captain admitted having thought up both practices and explained: "I felt that those women were guilty of an act of insubordination and that they had to be found out and punished as an example to the others."

"Are you satisfied that the way you acted on those occasions was proper?" the judge asked him.

"Yes, sir."

Instead of things settling down after the "lesson," another act of insubordination occurred.

Marta Henríquez Dorantes, the other woman who was allowed to leave the house to go to market with the Skeleton, was in the laundry shed wringing out clothes when she realized that several of her companions had entered and were standing around her, in silence, doing nothing that would explain why they were there.

She barely had time to become aware of their presence before they jumped her. Being four, they overcame her easily. They threw her to the floor, gagged her, and tied her arms and legs together with the wet clothes she had been washing, stood her up, and tried to kill her in a strange manner. There was an old outhouse in a corner of the yard that had been in disuse for many years. The women dragged Marta to this building, removed the boards covering the hole, and tried to stuff her into it. (The description of this deed leads to the conclusion that the attackers intended to bury their victim alive.) Her fatness saved her. Marta is a very broadly-built woman, and no matter how hard they tried, her assailants were unable to push her through the opening. They were engaged in the attempt when the Skeleton arrived.

This time the women were not punished, they were segregated. The Baladros decided that the four who had attacked Marta were to be taken to Los Pirules farm and shut up in the barn and the four who attacked Rosa should be locked in their rooms.

Considering that holding four women in solitary confinement called for vigilance during the night, Captain Bedoya assigned a trusted subaltern—Brave Nicolás—to stand guard, armed, and be at the orders of the Baladros in case anything came up.

XIV
What Teófilo Did

1

Teófilo Pinto, Eulalia Baladro's husband, is a taciturn individual with the morose expression of a man who has "worked honestly all his life without taking a vacation only to lose everything three times and end up in jail."

In explaining his actions, he states: As a business, Los Pirules farm was a failure. My sisters-in-law were to blame, because they did not turn the money over to me that they said they would. They promised to open a bank account in my name and deposit fifteen thousand pesos in it that I could draw on as needed and spend as I saw fit. Did you see that account? Did you see those fifteen thousand pesos? Well, neither did I.

They would send Ticho out every Saturday with just the exact amount to cover the payroll. I had to put up the money for any additional expenses out of my own pocket and then keep sending messages with Ticho to get them to pay me back.

The situation was bad enough right along, but toward the middle of October it got worse. Saturday came around, midday passed, and no sign of Ticho. The *peones* and I sat on the end of the irrigation ditch, watching the buses go by on the road without stopping to let off Ticho and his envelope of money. By the time the sun was going down, I couldn't stand the embarrassment any longer. I walked back to the house, took Eulalia's emergency savings out of the drawer, came back to where the *peones* were, and gave them each ten pesos.

"Be patient, boys," I told them. "I'll pay you the balance on Monday."

They went off, their heads bent, putting the money into their pockets.

I waited all day Sunday for word from my sisters-in-law, but nothing happened. I would have liked to go and talk to them to explain the situation, but they never would tell me where they were living.

The *peones* returned on Monday and worked for a while, but when midday came and Ticho did not appear with the money they knocked off and left. They came back later on Monday and again on Tuesday to collect, but I couldn't pay them, so that night they played me dirty.

I had covered the irrigation ditch with fourteen sheets of corrugated roofing paper to keep the water from seeping out and flooding the road. Well, when it looked like there was no hope of their ever collecting their wages, they came back during the night and carried off all the cardboard sheets.

When I got up the next morning and looked out of the window, the first thing I saw was the reflection off the water that covered the road. It wasn't hard to imagine who was to blame for the damage. You've really got to have it in for a person to come and carry off fourteen sheets of cardboard from such an out-of-the-way place.

I think the *peones* did something to the tractor, too, because on Thursday it stopped in the middle of the plowing and there was no way I could get it started.

I was desperate by the time I got back to the house.

"I have a good mind," I told my wife, "for us to pack up, go out on the highway, get on the first bus that comes by and ride to wherever it takes us, so as never to have to see this place or your sisters again."

That is what we should have done and didn't.

Eulalia did not want to offend her sisters and I didn't insist because I had hopes that they would pay up what they owed me. And, another thing, I wanted to see the wheat I had sown, sprout.

The following Monday, we were in the kitchen eating, when we heard a horn blowing as though somebody was calling for help. We went to the door and from there we saw the blue car my sisters-in-law always traveled in stuck in the puddle in the middle of the road. It was crammed with people.

I had to carry over stones and put them in the mud so Arcángela could get out of the car without dirtying her shoes. As soon as she stepped onto dry ground, I began complaining about her not sending the money for the *peones* and told her that they had left. She stopped me.

"Wait a minute," she said, "I've got something to tell you that's more important."

She made me walk a few steps with her to where she figured the people in the car wouldn't be able to hear. Then, she said to me, "There are four girls in the car who have behaved very badly. I want to separate them from the others before they get any ideas from them, so I am leaving them here for a few days to cool down!"

Then I realized that there were four women in the back of the car and they were looking at me in a very strange way. They were scared.

Arcángela gave me various instructions: "Keep them locked up. Give them whatever you want to eat. If you see any one of them trying to get away, take the rifle and shoot her."

2

The barn on Los Pirules farm is a long, narrow room with a cement floor, unfinished cinder block walls, and a concrete roof. The door is made of mesquite wood and is secured from the outside with a hasp and lock. There are iron bars across the transom set too close together for a body to squeeze between them. The light that filters through the transom is dim.

In preparing the barn to be occupied by the women, Teófilo removed anything at all that might be useful for escaping—an iron bar, a stool, a shovel. He left it empty except for a pile of straw and some corncobs.

Teófilo gave the women reed mats, which they laid out on the floor. They had brought blankets with them but suffered from the cold because the transom opening could not be closed and because it was a very sharp November—there had been four frosts. All the women caught cold, but recovered after a few days.

119

One of the inexplicable aspects of this story is how two people who prided themselves on their rectitude as much as the Pintos did could have lent themselves to serving as jailers without putting up the slightest objection. The answer might lie, at least partially, in the two thousand-peso check drawn on Arcángela's account that was cashed by Teófilo at the Pedrones bank on November 3. There is no evidence that he tried to hire other *peones* after that date. A good part of the land that had been plowed remained unplanted. Whatever farming was done Ticho was responsible for—the Baladros ordered that instead of carrying sacks he was to go out to the farm every morning "to see what should be attended to." It was Ticho who picked the ripened ears of corn, put them into sacks, and brought them into the house, and Ticho who put on rubber boots, took a shovel, and spent the day in the mud seeing to it that the recently sown wheat received water. Teófilo, meanwhile, was obsessed with getting the tractor started, spending hours puttering and cranking it, to no avail.

The four women spent three weeks in the barn, during which time, apparently, they were not ill-treated by either Teófilo or Eulalia. Their life was as follows: Teófilo would open the door early in the morning and let them out into the field for a while to do their wants and wash, if they wished, in the pond. After that he locked them up again. At around nine o'clock, he would open the door a second time and Eulalia would enter with dishes of food. The prisoners' breakfast consisted of tortillas, beans, chili pepper sauce, and a mug of orange-leaf tea. It was not very filling, but neither did it leave them too hungry. Eulalia returned for the dishes, which she washed herself. The women spent the rest of the day locked in. At six o'clock in the evening, Teófilo let them out into the field for another spell, after which they went back into the barn, had their supper consisting of the same food in the same amounts that they had had for breakfast, and after collecting the dishes, Teófilo locked the door and did not open it again until the next day.

The relations between the Pintos and the women were relatively cordial. Teófilo warned the prisoners: "There's no quarrel between you and us and we are not enemies. You have to stay here for a while because those are doña Arcángela's orders. The other orders she gave me were to see that you don't leave. Nobody has it in for you and you won't be lacking for anything here, so just behave yourselves and nobody will have any trouble."

One of the women ventured to ask how long they were going to be kept locked up, to which Teófilo replied, "As long as doña Arcángela says."

3

Ticho gets up before dawn—by choice, since he prefers spending the day out in the country to lugging sacks in a warehouse—and takes the first bus out of Concepción. His way of dressing is somewhere between that of a bouncer and a farmhand—undershirt with holes in it, a suit, rough sandals, and a broad-brimmed straw hat. He reaches the farm as day is breaking, while everybody is asleep except the dog, which does not bark at him. He puts on a pair of rubber boots that are under the shed and, shovel in hand, goes to check on the irrigation ditch to see what damage has been done and what progress the water has made during the night.

On the day and hour that concern us, Ticho was standing at the end of the irrigation ditch near the highway. What he saw can be imagined:

The road and the ditch run parallel in the direction away from him. The road is boggy with puddles and mud; the ditch is in a bank of earth covered with weeds. They divide the farm in two. On Ticho's right is the planted and watered field—an area of black earth with tiny green dots of wheat—and on his left is the ash-gray plowed but unsown surface, its furrows lumpy crags. At the other end of the ditch and road is the pond, next to it the barn and, next to the barn, the house. The house is painted white, has a porch and two windows; the barn is the color of cinder block and has one closed door. A few meters to the left of the house is the shed and under the shed, the tractor, which is red.

It is early morning, and cold. There is not a cloud in the sky.

A figure comes out on the porch of the house, goes to the barn and opens the big door. Four figures wrapped in rags come out of the barn, one by one, at unhurried intervals. They stand in the sun for a moment, then go to the fence, lift their skirts, and squat in a line. The figure that opened the door goes to the shed, leans over the front end of the tractor, makes a sudden movement with his arm, and a white puff of smoke appears at the other end above the exhaust pipe. Intermittent explosions are heard, then silence. Another figure appears on the porch of the house and remains there, motionless.

Ticho's attention wanders, he leans over the shovel, moves a chunk of earth aside to let the water run by, reinforces the edge of the ditch, and so forth. He does not raise his head again until he hears a shout.

The scene he now sees is different. The four women who had been squatting are now running over the plowed field. Ticho realizes that they are trying to cross diagonally to reach the highway at the point farthest away from where he is standing. The figure that was on the porch has disappeared, the one that was under the shed is moving toward the porch. The four figures crossing the furrows separate. The going is difficult, ankles twist, feet sink into the clumps of earth; they run but make little headway. The other two figures are now together in the portal. The one that went back into the house has come out again and is handing something to the one that has just arrived from the shed, who takes it in his two hands. This figure, standing straight, remains motionless a moment. Neither the flash nor the smoke can be seen. The reports take Ticho by surprise and startle him.

XV
The Run of
Bad Luck

1

"Señor don Teófilo says that the four women you left him in charge of tried to run away, so, like you ordered him he shot at them with the rifle you gave him for guarding the cows. One is already dead and one is dying. The other two gave up and we locked them in the barn again. That's how it is. Don Teófilo also says he is waiting for orders about what he should do now."

These, more or less, were the words with which Ticho broke the news to Arcángela scarcely an hour after the event. One can imagine what Arcángela said on hearing them. She did not admit at the time nor does she admit now ever having mentioned the word "rifle" in relation to the four women she brought to Los Pirules farm.

"I told him to keep an eye on them, to take care of them, that he should not let them get away, but not that he should shoot them."

At the present time, in speaking of Teófilo she invariably refers to him as "my brother-in-law, that horse's ass."

It should be pointed out that neither Ladder, who drove the women to the farm, nor Eulalia, who went out to the car with Teófilo when it was stuck in the mud, heard Arcángela mention the rifle.

It all adds up to the same thing: Arcángela gave Teófilo the rifle and brought the women to the farm and Teófilo shot at them in the conviction that he was carrying out Arcángela's orders.

Not long after hearing the news Arcángela began to feel ill—as she said, she got sick with anger—and had to take to her bed where the Skeleton brought her a mug of passionflower tea.

On that occasion, according to the Skeleton, Arcángela said to her, "It looks to me, little Skeleton, like we are really in the fucking soup now."

While Arcángela was recovering, Serafina and Ticho drove out to Los Pirules farm in Ladder's car. By the time they arrived, the wounded woman was dead.

Nobody recalls that Serafina reproached Teófilo for what he had done. She confined herself to taking the steps she thought advisable. She crossed the field with Ticho following behind balancing a pick and shovel on his shoulder until she came to what seemed to her to be a suitable spot. It was far from the highway at the foot of a little embankment shielded from indiscreet eyes— actually nobody was anywhere near—by cactuses. She ordered Ticho to dig there.

Serafina returned to the farmhouse as this work was being done. Having reached the conclusion that neither Teófilo nor her sister Eulalia was capable of "minding women," she had him open the barn, ordered the girls to come out, had them get into the car, and drove back to town with them. After seeing to it that they were each locked up in a room, she returned to the farm to super-vise the burial.

The dead women's clothing was put in a pile and set on fire. The bodies, wrapped in sacks, were carried from the shed—where they had been laid out—by Ticho, Lad-der, and Teófilo, who was reluctant, at first, to partici-pate in the grisly task. After Ladder and Ticho had filled in the grave and obliterated the traces as best they could, Serafina was satisfied. Night was falling and it was cold. Eulalia invited them in to have a bite to eat—the men were very hungry—but Serafina declined the invitation, saying that it was time to be getting back to town. They all went to the car and said goodbye there: Serafina kissed her sister, Teófilo opened the car door and, they say, asked his sister-in-law, "What do you want me to do, now?"

"Nothing," she answered. "When Arcángela feels better, she will decide what to do about you."

With that, they drove off toward Concepción. Teófilo and Eulalia remained alone on the farm with two crimes on their conscience, two bodies buried at the edge of the embankment fifty meters away, and the disturbing feeling that those who had given them work were dissatisfied with them.

2

Over the following weeks, the Casino del Danzón community was split and regrouped differently several times in accord with the obscure shifts in Arcángela's whim.

The four women who had beaten Rosa were segregated from the rest as though they had the plague. For a time, they lived locked up separately in the darkest rooms of the house. The Skeleton brought them food twice a day consisting of such meager portions of tortillas and beans that they were always left hungry. In contrast, the three who had not taken part in any attack and Marta had the run of the house and were free to go to the kitchen and fix themselves a bite any time they got hungry. The only restriction on the three girls was that they could not leave the house at all, while Marta was permitted exclusively to accompany the Skeleton to market. Rosa, still ill and unable to get out of bed, was relatively well taken care of. These women and their employers ate lightly but enough—unlimited amounts of beans and tortillas; vermicelli soup, occasionally; meat stew two or three times a week, especially when Captain Bedoya stayed for supper. Also, the Skeleton always served him an egg for breakfast which, as it passed by on a dish, was as close as the girls came to having one themselves. Brave Nicolás would arrive at nine o'clock. The captain had ordered him to use civilian clothes while on duty with the Baladros, but since he owned few he would turn up most nights wearing a regulation army shirt on which the faded number of his regiment could be distinguished. The Skeleton pampered him. She would serve him two eggs drowned in *mulato* chili pepper sauce, a tall pile of tortillas, and a mug of orange-leaf tea in order that, as the Skeleton would say, he should be able to resist "the chills" better. Supposedly, the Brave Man was standing guard to prevent the four prisoners from escaping. Actually, he wrapped himself in his army coat and slept soundly, propped across the staircase, halfway up, with an automatic rifle beside him.

The situation changed after Teófilo killed the two girls. The two surviving participants of the escape attempt dropped to the bottom of the whorehouse ladder. They were treated like criminals for having witnessed the killing of their companions, shut up in "sealed" rooms, given food that consisted of leftovers from the plates of the others, which amounted to practically nothing, and never allowed to go out. These two were so effectively isolated that the rest of the girls living in the house had no idea until several months later that they were there, nor were they aware of what had happened at the farm.

In contrast to the punishment and solitary confinement suffered by the women who were brought back from the farm, Arcángela decided to reduce the sentence of the four who had attacked Rosa—even though she had still not recovered—and permitted them to come out of their rooms during the day, have their meals in the kitchen, eat their fill, be together, and talk to the others. After supper, they had to return to their rooms where the Skeleton would lock them in until the next day.

It appears that this act of locking a door at night and opening it in the morning earned the Skeleton the enmity of the captives with whom she had been on relatively friendly terms up to that time, even though there was not the slightest doubt that she was unconditionally with the Baladros and, consequently, against the rebels.

It seems that there was neither provocation nor quarrel. What the four women expected to accomplish is unknown. The incident was like this: One morning after breakfast, the four women were in the kitchen washing dishes when the Skeleton came in. She states that the moment she entered she realized that they were waiting for her; they maintain that they had not been in collusion. The Skeleton claims that she did not even open her mouth; they claim that she insulted them, saying "What the fuck!" (?) The fact of the matter is that before the Skeleton could defend herself, Aurora Bautista struck her in the face with a clay dish, breaking it, and another of the girls—the victim does not know which— hit her over the head with the big wooden spoon.

Everything seems to indicate that the intention of these four women was to do the same to the Skeleton as the other four had tried to do to Marta: push her into the hole of the old outhouse and bury her alive. It should be noted that this attempt had a better chance of succeeding than the other, because the Skeleton, being so much thinner than Marta, would have fitted into the hole.

Fortunately for all concerned, the attempt was thwarted. The women were crossing the yard carrying the semiconscious Skeleton when they met Arcángela on her way back to the house from feeding the chickens. What happened then is a demonstration of the power still wielded by a madam over her girls, even at that time. They were so dismayed at seeing her that they were powerless to do anything but obey. Without so much as bothering to put down the dish she held in her hand, Arcángela made the four women carry the Skeleton back to her room, lay her on her bed, and call Serafina—who was in the dining room—to lock them in.

Captain Bedoya supervised the punishment that night. He made the four guilty girls beat each other with the wooden spoon. It was on this occasion that Aurora Bautista, seized by some obscure impulse, struck Socorro in the mouth several times, breaking two of her teeth. María del Carmen screamed, "You're killing her!" and the captain intervened, snatching the spoon away from Aurora. (At the trial, the captain brought up this act of humanitarianism on his part.)

The Skeleton, whose face remained swollen for more than a week, did not participate in the punishment that night nor did she show any signs afterward of holding a grudge against her assailants.

Captain Bedoya had to go to Mezcala on army business in the middle of December. He took two points into consideration in planning the trip: first, that the price of a hotel room is practically the same if you sleep alone or with somebody; and, second, that with life at the Casino del Danzón getting more and more dismal, and Serafina having been under constant nervous tension for months, she deserved a change. The captain invited her to accompany him, and she accepted.

They went in the first-class bus. The captain was gallant. He allowed Serafina to have the seat next to the window; and—something else he would never have done for anybody—he got off the bus at one of the rest stops and bought her some candied crab apples that had caught her attention, which he paid for himself. The captain was in uniform; Serafina wore a red kerchief on her head to keep her hair from getting mussed.

The captain says that as soon as the bus was on the highway Serafina seemed to forget the problems of the house, to relax and become absorbed in watching the scenery, which evoked frequent comments from her, such as "Look at that beautiful field!" or "I wonder what it must feel like to live in a lonely place like that!" All of which, in the captain's opinion, clearly indicated Serafina's intention at the time of getting out of prostitution and taking up farming.

They arrived in the city of Mezcala at eight o'clock in the evening. The captain continued to be indulgent. He rejected the idea of staying at one of the hotels near the bus terminal, considering them "reasonable in price but in a very noisy location." They took a taxi—which he paid for—to a relatively deluxe hotel in the downtown area. The captain did not become annoyed even when the desk clerk told him the prices of the rooms. He insisted on seeing several so Serafina could choose the one she liked best. They finally decided on a room that overlooked a little park with benches and the atrium of a church.

Serafina removed her red kerchief and the captain took her to a popular beer garden for supper.

The next day, the captain spent the best part of the morning at the quartermaster general's office. Serafina went to the arcade and bought some typical Mezcala candies as a gift for her sister. At midday, on his way back to the hotel, the captain caught sight of her from a distance, leaning over the balcony railing, waving and smiling at him. He says that he had not seen her so happy in a long time.

After dinner they went to a movie and after the movie they parted, the captain returning to headquarters and Serafina strolling back to the hotel. She describes what happened in the following way. Toward dusk, she was walking along a street the name of which she does not recall. There were many people around. Suddenly, she relates, something on the other side of the street attracted her attention, she could not say exactly what—a silhouette, a gesture—and gave her an uneasy feeling. She says that she kept walking, without knowing what was happening to her at first, and that it took a while before she realized that she had seen Simón Corona in the crowd. All the suppressed anger of years welled up in her, a bitter taste came into her mouth, and she had to stop to spit. She says that she felt the same humiliation all over again of the night in Acapulco when she went into the store, so worried, saw the other door, and realized that Simón Corona had tricked her. And she says that once again she began to feel sorry for herself —she who had been so good to him, to be paid back so ungratefully. She thinks that if she had had the .45 in her purse she would have shot into the crowd of people across the street. But she did not have it with her.

She says that she became as though crazed. She ran across the street dodging the cars, hit a fat man in the stomach who got in her way, raced down the block as far as the corner and stood there, staring in all directions, but saw no sign anywhere of the man she hated so much.

She says that she walked up and down streets without knowing where she was going until finally she had to ask directions to get back to the hotel. It was during this lapse of wandering about lost that her desire for revenge was rekindled.

"It is not possible that such a terrible offense should go unpunished! It is not fair!"

Captain Bedoya says that when he got back to the hotel, he found Serafina transformed. Instead of her being out on the balcony leaning over the railing as he expected, when he opened the door he saw her sitting in a chair in a corner of the room, almost in darkness. She stared at him. Obviously, she was waiting for him. He had scarcely set foot in the room before she was saying, "There is something in my life you don't know about."

One can imagine the captain taking off his jacket, going into the bathroom and urinating with the door open, as Serafina, standing in the center of the room, relates the story in a voice charged with emotion of her relations with Simón Corona—of whose existence the captain knew nothing—with the words "skunk," "ingrate," "unforgivable," and the like coming up frequently, and ending with her saying, "It was to kill that man that I wanted the .45 pistol you sold me."

What happened after that is surprising: Captain Bedoya, instead of telling Serafina that she was talking nonsense and to try to calm down and forget the whole thing, agreed that she was right and promised to help her take revenge.

Apparently, Serafina spent the next day scouring Mezcala in search of Simón Corona. She did not find him—it was later learned that he was not present in that city at the time—and that what Serafina had seen in the street was an illusion. It cost the captain some effort to convince her to go back to Concepción. She did not relent in her determination to take vengeance and held the captain to his promise and so, a few days later, Serafina, the captain, Brave Nicolás, and Ladder set out for Tuxpana Falls. (See Chapter I.)

During the trial, Captain Bedoya maintained that the purpose of the trip to Tuxpana Falls was "to throw a scare into Simón Corona," not to kill him, as might have been suspected from the number of shots pumped into the bakery by Serafina and Brave Nicolás with lethal-caliber arms. The Brave Man's statement jibes with the captain's—he claims to be an excellent marksman and that he would have had no problem in hitting his target if he had wanted to. Serafina, however, in reply to the judge's question "Do you think that this man—Simón

Corona—deserved to be killed for having left you standing on a street corner waiting for him when he had no intention of returning?" answered yes and admitted later that she aimed at him from the bakery door but that the .45 "did not obey her."

XVI
Enter the Police

1

"Do you suspect who might have been responsible for the attack?" the agent of the attorney general's office of Tuxpana Falls asked Simón Corona, who was lying, bandaged, on a cot in the first aid station.

Simon answered instantly that it was Serafina. On being asked for information regarding the presumably guilty party, he gave the address of the Molino Street house, being unaware of the existence of the Casino del Danzón.

The investigation went through bureaucratic channels from that point on, having been converted into official papers that lay for days in one desk drawer or another, multiplied, returned to their office of origin, were reissued, arrived at another office, remained in other desk drawers for further periods. In this case, it is hard to know which is more remarkable, the tortuousness of justice or its infallibility. The bureaucratic procedures were finalized with the arrival at the desk of the chief of police of Concepción, Teódulo Cueto, of a memorandum that said: "Kindly place señora Serafina Baladro Juárez at the disposition of the attorney general's office of the state of Mezcala," and so forth.

The first thing the chief of police did upon receiving this order was to meet with Captain Bedoya in the Gómez Hotel bar. Chief Cueto denies that such a meeting took place. Captain Bedoya, on the other hand, described what was said during it, as follows:

He told me that he was notifying me that he had received a warrant of arrest for Serafina and that it would be a good idea for her to have a lawyer on tap. I told him that I could not imagine why there should be a warrant for Serafina and even less why she should need a lawyer. The chief then told me that there had been a shooting in Tuxpana Falls and that her name appeared in the official record. On hearing this, I answered, "Chief, I give you my oath as an officer of the Mexican Army and on the honor of my sainted mother that Serafina knows nobody in Tuxpana Falls, has never set foot in that town, does not know where it is or, probably, even that it exists."

The chief said that he appreciated my frankness and that he was certain there was no criminal charge against Serafina, but that he would have to take her into custody, nonetheless. I thanked him for giving me the tip. He told me that in accordance with the instructions he had received, he would have to break the seals on the Casino del Danzón the next day and check over the interior of the premises. He told me he felt sure that he would find everything in order, after which we said good night.

Captain Bedoya got to the Casino as fast as he could. The news, naturally, caused consternation. The Skeleton says that Arcángela reproached Serafina, saying, "All on account of you and your selfishness! You had to get your revenge and now we are ruined!"

Serafina answered, "Is it my fault I was born hot-blooded?"

Orders went flying through the house and there was general mobilization. Ticho mixed mortar in the dining room and began to close up the opening in the wall. Ladder was summoned. The women were ordered to pack up blankets and dishes for spending the night at Los Pirules farm. Serafina tried to locate *licenciado* Rendón who disappears from the story at this point. The Baladros tried to get in touch with him more than thirty times over the next two weeks without success. Moments of vacillation were not wanting. At one point, Serafina suggested to her sister before witnesses, "Let's go to the United States."

But they went to the farm. Ladder made four trips in

his car that afternoon. The eleven remaining girls were together once more. They laid down reed mats in the barn and went to sleep in apparent harmony, with the Skeleton on guard. It was cold. In the morning, Rosa was found to have a high fever. The Skeleton diagnosed it as a chill and gave her marjoram tea. Rosa drank it, seemed to improve, and died three hours later. Ticho buried her at the foot of the embankment in a grave that he dug hurriedly next to the other two.

2

The next day, January 14, Chief Cueto broke the seals on the Independence Street house and entered with three uniformed officers and a marshal. Apparently, they made a tour of the house and found nothing that seemed irregular to them. The police spent barely fifteen minutes in the building. The official report of the inspection of the premises omits any reference to the fact that the tortillas found in the kitchen could not have been there for two years.

Chief Cueto went to Los Pirules farm that same afternoon. The water had seeped out of the irrigation ditch, the road was soft and muddy, and his car got stuck. While the three policemen and the marshal were trying to free it, the inspector walked the two hundred meters to the house. Arcángela and Serafina were standing on the porch as though they were expecting him. Chief Cueto states that before he could even say good morning, Arcángela said to him, "It will be worth ten thousand pesos to you if you report that you couldn't locate my sister."

What the chief replied is not known. (The Baladros never said that they had offered or gave him money.) That night the chief wrote a report, which he sent to headquarters, stating that he broke the seals on the Casino del Danzón, inspected the interior of the premises, and visited Los Pirules farm "without finding the wanted person." The terms in which the document is couched are definitive. Anybody unfamiliar with the story who read it might assume that the investigation must have ended at that point.

This was not the case. Chief Cueto returned to the Casino del Danzón the following day accompanied by the three uniformed policemen and the marshal, as on the previous occasion.

(It should be noted that Chief Cueto's motives for returning to the Casino del Danzón are as obscure as those for his having warned Captain Bedoya in their conversation at the Gómez Hotel that he was about to make an arrest. He gives the following explanation for his actions: "The amount señora Arcángela offered me was so large that it made me suspect that the señoras Baladro had something more serious on their consciences than the shooting up of the bakery in Tuxpana Falls in which no loss of life or serious casualties were involved. That was the reason I decided to return to the Casino del Danzón and make a more thorough inspection.")

On their second visit to the Casino del Danzón, Chief Cueto and his men went through the rooms, up and down the stairs, in and out of the cabaret, checked over the kitchen and the charcoal shed, and finally ended up in the yard. Countless traces of recent occupation must have turned up, but that was not what interested them. The chief paced back and forth over the yard.

All at once—he states—"I noticed that my feet sank into the ground in a certain spot. I called one of the officers who was with me and told him to get a shovel and dig a hole right there where I was standing. I wanted to see what was underneath."

When the officer had dug down about one meter, what was left of one of Blanca's hands appeared.

3

After this sensational discovery, there is a gap of several hours. Chief Cueto sends to Pedrones for reinforcements and waits for them to arrive before taking the next step. He loses more time later taking precautions: one squad of riflemen south of Los Pirules farm to cut off access to the highway; another squad to the north to cover the rear, and so on. The chief is the first to reach the house. He wears a Stetson hat, bulletproof vest, and carries a pistol. The house is empty. When the police break open the barn door, most of the women whom they find inside complain of not having eaten in twenty-four hours.

One of the prisoners—Aurora Bautista—reports having overheard the Baladros say the word "Nogales." On hearing this, he moves fast for the first time. He orders the women who were in the barn to be taken to headquarters while he and two policemen get into their car and drive at full speed to Pedrones.

They reach the terminal in time to hold up a bus about to depart in the direction of Nogales. Chief Cueto climbs aboard and stands in the aisle looking around. Seat numbers 23 and 24 are occupied by two women with shawls over their faces, apparently asleep. They are the Baladro sisters.

4

When the Baladros reached the Concepción police headquarters, they were led along a corridor onto which opened the office where the girls who had been rescued from the barn were making their statements. It is said that when the two women passed by in custody, several of them got to their feet and shouted insults at them, the first the sisters had ever received from their employees.

Captain Bedoya and Serafina had arranged to meet in Nogales. Unaware that the Baladros had been arrested, he slept on the post, got up early, held inspection, had breakfast at the Gómez Hotel, and reached the Plan de Abajo Commercial Bank as it was opening.

The captain was filling out a withdrawal slip with which to close out his savings account when two detectives entered the bank to arrest him. They went up to him and, in a low voice, so as not to attract the employees' attention, one of them said to him, "My Captain, you are under arrest."

The detective states that Captain Bedoya did not blink an eye on hearing this. He tore up the withdrawal slip, put his pen back in his pocket, and held out his wrists to be handcuffed. The detectives carried no handcuffs and the three men left the bank arm in arm like old friends pleased to have run into one another.

Brave Nicolás, who did not think he was guilty of anything, was arrested in the barracks. Ladder, who also considered himself innocent, was arrested two days later while seated on the fence of the San Francisco church atrium discussing the case of the Baladros with the other taxi drivers. Nobody had denounced Ticho and he was not wanted by the authorities. He gave himself up voluntarily when he learned that the Baladros were in jail. He practically had to insist that the police lock him up. Eulalia and Teófilo Pinto would have escaped, because the police had no photographs of them, had it not occurred to them to cross the border "to reach safety." They were detained in Texas for traveling without a passport and turned over to the Mexican authorities to whom they gave their real names.

The Concepción jail—which usually housed only the drunks who were freed in the morning after sweeping the streets—for the first time held nineteen prisoners.

A few days later there were twenty inmates: Simón Corona was brought in from Tuxpana Falls for questioning. However, he did not spend even one day there since another prisoner, it is not known who, stabbed him—not fatally—and he had to be hospitalized.

5

Chief Cueto's role in the apprehension of the Baladro sisters is one of the obscure parts of this story. The following hypothesis seems reasonable.

At the outset, Chief Teódulo Cueto, whose name appears in the section of Arcángela's notebook headed "Payments" (See Appendix, § 6), tried to do his duty while at the same time giving the Baladros opportunities to escape—he tips off Captain Bedoya in the Gómez Hotel bar; he enters the Casino at a time when nobody is there; when he finds the woman whom he has orders to arrest, he does not take her into custody. It is possible that he accepted the ten thousand pesos Arcángela offered him, not to close the case for an indefinite time, but only to give them two days' head start. It is also possible that after collecting, the chief may have changed his mind—when Blanca's hand was uncovered in the yard, for instance—and decided to speed up the proceedings and make the arrest. The Baladros would have needed twenty-four hours more to make good their escape.

It must be granted that this hypothesis does not account for the chief's discovery of Blanca's body on his second visit to the Casino del Danzón, which may have come about purely by chance.

XVII
Judge Peralta's Justice

1

When Judge Peralta was assigned to preside over the trial of "Serafina and Arcángela Baladro, et al.," his first concern was to divide the nineteen suspects into two groups. Those who complained of mistreatment in their preliminary statements were considered victims and those who had nothing to complain about were presumed to be the guilty parties.

His second step was to have the innocent and guilty groups separated from each other. The six victims were taken from their cell to a room without bars that had been prepared for them in the courthouse building. It faced on the inside patio and was furnished with beds provided by various Christian families. These women were given permission to leave the building by the judge who reminded them of their duty to be available for all judicial acts. He also excused them from eating the food prepared by the jailer's wife—which, by general agreement, was abominable—and money was collected by a group of Concepción citizens, headed by the mayor, to pay a woman who ran a lunchroom in the market to send in breakfast and the midday meal for six each day in dinner pails. The public was concerned about the health of the women, who had declared in their state-

139

ments that they had not had enough to eat in over a year.

"Just you wait until our influential friends find out what you are doing to us and you'll see who is right," Arcángela said when the marshal read out the accusations against them that appeared in the official record.

Two days passed. No influential friends came forward and the Baladros were unable even to communicate with *licenciado* Rendón. When this became evident, three of the girls who had made no complaints requested permission from the judge to add to their statements that when they began to work for the Baladro sisters they had been hoodwinked with respect to what the job entailed (two of them came to the Molino Street house under the impression that they were going to be servants and the third thought it was a match factory), that they had been under age, had stayed on against their wills (ten, twelve, and fifteen years, respectively), and had never received payment for their services.

The day they made these emendations to their statements, the three women were taken out of their cell and treated as victims from then on.

2

At first, the Baladros refused to make any statement without consulting their attorney. But, time passed and *licenciado* Rendón never appeared, so, finally, they had no choice but to submit to preliminary questioning without counsel:

Q: How do you account for the presence of three corpses in the yard of your house?

A: We have no idea. There is no telling how they could have gotten there.

Q: Several of the female employees complain that you were starving them. They say that all you gave them to eat was one tortilla and five beans each. What do you have to say to that?

A: It is a lie. We gave them the same as people eat all over. Even vermicelli soup.

Four days after the apprehension, columnists wrote in various newspapers that the Baladros were so influential in the state of Plan de Abajo that it would be impossible to convict them. In reply to this allegation, Judge Peralta placed a temporary embargo on all properties belonging to the sisters "for the purpose of protecting the means of compensating the victims."

Arcángela fainted when she received this news.

"They want to take our property away from us," she said when she came to.

A photograph of her appeared in the newspapers, her hands gripping the bars as though she wanted to break them, over a caption that read: "Responsible for six deaths and all she thinks about is her property."

Since the Baladros' lawyer showed no signs of putting in an appearance, Judge Peralta appointed *licenciado* Gedeón Céspedes to defend them.

The *licenciado* was interviewed by the press after having met with the defendants. "Don't get me wrong," he told the reporters, "the only reason I am defending these women is because I have to. It is my duty as a public defense counsellor, but I have no sympathy for them. On the contrary, I believe they deserve to get death, a penalty which I regret to say does not exist in the state of Plan de Abajo."

3

". . . that they forbade her to leave the house; that they gave her hardly anything to eat; and that one time when she and three of the girls did something the señoras did not like, the four of them were locked up in a room and then Serafina came in and said to the declarant, 'Here is the stick. Take it and beat them with it. And you better hit hard because if I see that you don't, I will hit you myself.'" (She exhibits bruises.)

". . . that he saw señora Arcángela Baladro unwrap a package that was on the table. It was the rifle; that the aforementioned then said the following words: 'I am leaving you this rifle to defend yourself with in case somebody tries to steal the cows' . . . and that the same señora Baladro said to him on another occasion: 'I am putting these four girls in your charge. Keep a close watch on them. If you catch any one of them trying to get away, shoot her with the rifle I left you to guard the cows with.' That is why the declarant says he was only obeying orders when he shot."

Concerning the guilt of Captain Bedoya:

". . . that while the declarant was washing clothes in the laundry tubs together with some of the other girls, she saw Captain Bedoya come into the yard and walk to the back wall unbuttoning his trousers with the idea of urinating when he stopped short and stood there looking at the tub under the lemon tree. 'What's that?' he asked them and they answered, 'It's Blanca,' which put him into a bad temper and he said to señora Serafina, 'Tell Ticho to carry Blanca out to the garbage dump at the edge of town and leave her there for the dogs to eat.'"

". . . that she saw Captain Bedoya cut switches off a bush in the yard and hit them against the palm of his hand to see which hurt the most . . ."

". . . that when she was waiting on the table she heard the captain say to señora Serafina: 'These women you got here are no good anymore, their meat is all flabby. The only way they might interest somebody is in tacos with *mole* sauce . . .'"

". . . that she hasn't the slightest doubt that Captain Bedoya was Serafina Baladro's man and that he sometimes slept with her since on various occasions that the declarant waited on table in the dining room she saw the said captain taking off his belt after supper . . ."

". . . that in the mornings the captain had an egg for breakfast which those who were in the kitchen would see being carried out."

These statements and others like them constituted the evidence on which Judge Peralta charged Captain Bedoya with complicity in the crimes and having been the brain behind them.

The charges against the Skeleton were:

". . . that when they reached Los Pirules farm, one of the girls, named Rosa X, took very sick and that the declarant saw that the woman whose nickname was the Skeleton came over to the said Rosa and said to her, 'I'll make you some tea'; that later she put water to boil on the brazier and threw various ingredients into the pot but that she did not know what they were; that she saw the aforementioned Skeleton pour the tea into a mug and serve it to the sick girl who died a few hours later and was buried in a hole that the person known as Ticho dug in the ground."

". . . that she—the Skeleton—was permitted to go out on the street but we were not, and that she made the meals but we were not even allowed to light the fire . . ."

". . . that she—the Skeleton—was the one who gave Blanca the Coca-Cola to drink that killed her . . ."

The record contains no reference to the attempt by the four women to bury the Skeleton alive in the old outhouse.

The charges against Ladder were:

". . . that when they were going to be moved from San Pedro de las Corrientes to Concepción, the declarant and another woman were sitting in the car next to the driver whose nickname is Ladder, who opened the door on their side and said, 'You can fit in here, Captain.' And the captain sat down squeezing the women and making them feel as though they were going to smother; that, on the same occasion the declarant said, 'I feel like my bones are going to break,' but nobody paid any attention . . ."

The foregoing paragraph indicates that Ladder broke the traffic laws of the state of Plan de Abajo on two counts: transportation of passengers under conditions dangerous to health, and transportation of prostitutes within the territory of a state in which prostitution is illegal. Simón Corona's statement (see Chapter II) cast suspicion on him of having transported corpses.

And so on.

On the fifth day of the trial, Aurora Bautista requested the judge for permission to change her statement as follows: Where it says "they made up the accounts each month and deducted the expenses from what she earned, but during the last year they neither kept accounts nor gave her anything . . ." to read "they made up accounts every month but never gave her anything . . ."

Where it says "She was nineteen years old when she came to work in the Molino Street house" to read "She does not remember exactly how old she was, but she thinks she was sixteen years of age."

She also requests—the record says—to add the following: "that she saw the sisters Serafina and Arcángela Baladro push the two women who fell off the balcony on September 14."

4

The first report of the case of the Baladro sisters appeared on page 8 of the *Abajo Sun* in the "News from Concepción" section. When it came out that the three bodies discovered were of young women and that they were found in a brothel, the story was spread over the front pages of all the papers in the country. On the third day, an avid public was informed of the discovery of three more bodies at Los Pirules farm.

Concepción became jammed with reporters, photographers, and sensation seekers. At the time he reconstructed the crimes, Judge Peralta counted 119 persons in the courtroom who had no good reason to be there. The confrontation between Serafina Baladro and Aurora Bautista, at which the two women exchanged insults and called each other liar, was held under the lenses of twenty-three cameras. At the photographers' request, the victims—nine by that time—posed kneeling on the floor of the little patio next to the kitchen with their arms outstretched at their sides, holding stones similar to the ones gathered by Captain Bedoya.

The newspapermen and the public in general hoped that more bodies would turn up. This fascination influenced evaluation of the events. For instance, Simón Corona's statement in which he declared that he helped the Baladro sisters transport a body to the mountain in 1960 gave rise to the belief that the Baladro sisters had devoted themselves for years to murdering women and throwing their bodies by roadsides or burying them in a corner of their yard. The victims wracked their memories and came up with such testimony as this, which appeared in the newspapers: "I recall a woman by the name of Patricia who worked in the México Lindo for a few days and then disappeared and nobody ever heard anything of her again . . ." and so on. The authorities of San Pedro de las Corrientes ordered the floor of the México Lindo torn up to see if there were any bodies buried there; nothing was found. More than thirty letters were received at the *Abajo Sun* from mothers who had lost touch with one or more of their daughters whom they had reason to suspect were in houses of prostitution and asking the editor of the paper to please let them know if any of the corpses or living victims looked like the girl in the enclosed photograph.

Chief Cueto made a final attempt to uncover other bodies. He took five of the defendants, Captain Bedoya, Ladder, Teófilo Pinto, Ticho, and Brave Nicolás out of prison and brought them under escort to the Casino del Danzón. He led them all into the cabaret, handed each a pick and shovel, and ordered them to dig up the floor, with a warning that work would not be stopped until a body was found. (His purpose in giving this order—Chief Cueto explained to the reporters—was to induce one of the defendants to confess where a body was buried instead of digging indefinitely in a spot where he knew there was nothing.) Since none of the accused confessed, the five dug for three full days, first in the cabaret—leaving the hole that may be seen to this day —then in the yard, and finally in the plowed field at Los Pirules farm in a spot picked at random by the chief.

Judge Peralta found "Serafina and Arcángela Baladro, et al." guilty on the following counts: first-degree murder; negligent homicide; illegal deprivation of freedom; physical and moral mistreatment; illegal possession of firearms; illegal carrying of idem; threats with idem; corruption of minors; pandering; deprivation of earnings of a third party; deceitful representation; illegal occupancy of attached property; illegal burial; violation of federal and state traffic laws; and concealment of assets.

The judge, therefore, passed sentence, as follows: Serafina and Arcángela Baladro, thirty-five years imprisonment, for multiple crimes; Captain Bedoya, twenty-five years imprisonment, for complicity and instigation of idem; the Skeleton, twenty years imprisonment, for first-degree murder (of Rosa X) and for negligent homicide (of Blanca X); Teófilo Pinto, twenty years for two first-degree homicides; Eulalia Baladro, his wife, fifteen years for taking the rifle off the wall and handing it to her husband; Ticho, twelve years, for illegal burial and complicity in multiple crimes; Ladder, six years for violation of traffic laws and complicity in the crimes, and so on.

Judge Peralta ordered that the attached properties of the Baladro sisters be sold in sufficient quantity to satisfy the compensations that he himself calculated. An example follows:

Calculation of compensation of Blanca X:

For back pay due (for ten years work at the rate of 300 pesos per month, the minimum wage	36,000.00 pesos
For accrued interest	18,000.00 pesos
For death of the worker	10,000.00 pesos
	64,000.00 pesos

This amount was deposited with the court at the disposal of any person able to substantiate his claim to being her legitimate heir. (It has remained unclaimed.)

There was a turkey-in-*mole*-sauce fiesta in the court-house patio on the day the nine surviving victims received their compensations from Judge Peralta. The women were photographed first being handed their checks, then, eating, and, finally, kneeling in the Concepción church thanking God for having made it possible for them to get out of their predicament alive. By the time they were finished praying, the photographers had left. The women said goodbye to one another in the atrium and each went her way. Dusk was falling. Nothing was ever heard of any of them again.

Epilogue

Simón Corona recovered completely from the knifing in prison, served his time in a state of Mezcala penitentiary where he was a model prisoner and, after being released, returned to Tuxpana Falls where he opened a bakery and lives happily. Of the others who are free, Brave Nicolás is now a shoemaker—a trade he learned in jail; Ticho has a steady job in the Barajas Brothers' warehouse; Ladder went back to his former occupation and now owns a fleet of taxis in San Pedro de las Corrientes—bought, as the gossip goes, with money given him by Arcángela.

Teófilo won a fortune in jail playing Spanish rummy and then lost it. Eulalia, who is free, sells coconut candies on the street. Captain Bedoya is in the Pedrones penitentiary where he is a trusty in charge of a cell block and highly regarded by both guards and prisoners. The Baladros are still in the women's prison from which they have no expectation of coming out alive. Serafina has a soft-drink business—charging exorbitant prices—and Arcángela sells food prepared by the Skeleton. Both are also moneylenders and have a joint capital estimated by the other prisoners at upwards of a hundred thousand pesos.

Appendix

1. Ticho's life as told by him.

When I was a small boy, the other children were afraid
of me. My parents sent me to school but the teacher did
not want me. She said I was too big and might set a bad
example. They put me to work carrying—stones, bags of
cement, bags of sand. One afternoon, I gave a friend of
mine a hug and when I let loose of him he fell down to
the ground. The people who saw what happened said I
killed him. So they put me in jail. In jail, they had me
carrying stones again. Then, the man who carried the
dead bodies in the hospital died himself and the doctor
came to the jail to look for somebody to take his place.
The director of the jail sent for me and said to me: "Go
along with this man." I carried stiffs back and forth for
ten years until one morning the doctor said to me, "You
can go, now," and he opened the hospital gate. I went
out on the street and started walking. I came to the rail-
road tracks and began to follow them. I walked at night
because there was a moon. In the daytime, I lay in a
ditch and slept. When I saw a house I would go to the
kitchen—dogs never bark at me—and I would peek in
and say to the women there, "I'm hungry," and they
would get scared and give me food. When I came to a
town I would beg but nobody gave. One day I was asleep
on the sidewalk outside a market and when I opened my
eyes doña Arcángela was looking down at me. There
were two girls with her carrying baskets. Doña Arcángela said to me, "You sure are big, you are homely as
sin, and you look like a dunce. I have a job for you you
will like."

The girls laughed.

From that day on I was a bouncer. My duties were to sit in a chair and be ready for whatever came up.

2. The Whoremaster's statement.

He states that it was intellectual curiosity that impelled him to go to the México Lindo so often. He describes some of the more noteworthy women he knew in that house. One, who undressed in great embarrassment four or five times every night saying that no man had ever seen her naked before. Another had sexual relations with the narrator on more than twenty occasions and never once recognized him. Another always told the same story: She had just received a telegram saying that her mother had taken sick and needed money urgently, and so forth.

The most interesting part of my visits—says The Whoremaster—would be the conversations I had with doña Arcángela who always had me sit at her table. She was a philosopher. For example, she believed that after you died your soul remained floating in the atmosphere for a length of time that depended on the memory you left behind in the minds of those who knew you. A bad memory made the soul suffer; a good one gave it joy. When everybody has forgotten the dead person or when all those who knew him have died, the soul disappears.

3. What the judo champion said.

I was among those chosen to represent Mexico City in the Pan American Judo Championships, which were held in the city of Pedrones in 1958. (He describes the accommodations provided them, his impression of the city, and how the Mexico City team was eliminated in the first round, after which they went to the México Lindo.) When the girls found out that we were the Mexico City judo team, they crowded around our table asking for autographs. The madam (Serafina) came over to shake hands with us, had the girls put wreaths of paper flowers around our necks, and gave us a drink on the house.

"Boys, a toast to your victory!" she said to us.

We didn't have the heart to tell her we had already been eliminated. (He describes the place, makes a comparison between Mexico City and Pedrones prostitutes, finding that the latter are less expensive and more sincere than the former, relates his experiences with a girl named Magdalena, and regrets that the Molino Street house was closed before he had a chance to pay it another visit.)

4. Statement of Don Gustavo Hernández.

Ask me: What is a man doing in a whorehouse every Saturday night when he has a wife and several daughters and a happy home life? I wouldn't know what to answer you, but that's how it was—I was like under a spell. Every Saturday night, as soon as the church clock struck nine, I would close my haberdashery shop and go to the México Lindo. The minute I set foot inside the place everything seemed beautiful to me: the decorations, the girls, the music. I didn't miss a thing. I danced, I drank, I talked, and there wasn't a woman who came through there between '57 and '60 that I didn't have.

I would get home with the first rays of the sun. "Where were you?" my wife would ask. "At a Catholic Action meeting." She never believed me. For years she suspected I had a mistress. She doesn't know I deceived her with forty-three women.

Doña Arcángela would say to me, "Don Gustavo, don't deny yourself anything. If you don't have the cash on you, just sign. You are as good as the Bank of Mexico for me."

Those words were my downfall. One morning, *licenciado* Rendón walked into the haberdashery store. In his briefcase he had IOUs signed by me for over fourteen thousand pesos. He wanted to know when I was going to pay up.

Doña Arcángela took my haberdashery shop away from me, but I got a scare that cured me of the vice and I never feel tempted to go to a whorehouse anymore. I live a contented life now with my family.

5. The photo.

1. Arcángela Baladro
2. The Skeleton
3. Serafina Baladro
4. Blanca (died, July 17)

154

5. Evelia (died, September 14)
6. Feliza (ditto)
7. Rosa (died, January 15)
8. Marta (did not fit into the outhouse hole)
9. Aurora Bautista (received compensation)
10 and 11. The women killed by Teófilo Pinto

6. Arcángela's notebook.

Arcángela's notebook was found in her room in the Casino del Danzón. It has three sections. The first contains the weekly balance sheet of the employees which has been described in Chapter IX.

The second section is headed "Due from Customers." It contains the names of the most respectable citizens of San Pedro de las Corrientes, the dates of their IOUs, interest at the rate of 10 percent per month, payments on account, and so forth. All these accounts have been liquidated.

The third section is headed "Payments." This consists of an itemized list of the amounts Arcángela was paying out to the authorities to be at peace with the township. For example, ten pesos daily to the policemen on the block, sixty to the mayor, sixty to the chief of police, and so on.

AVON BARD
DISTINGUISHED
LATIN AMERICAN FICTION

■By Jorge Amado

DONA FLOR AND HER TWO HUSBANDS	54031-2/$3.95
GABRIELA, CLOVE AND CINNAMON	60525-2/$4.95
HOME IS THE SAILOR	45187-5/$2.75
SHEPHERDS OF THE NIGHT	58768-8/$3.95
TENT OF MIRACLES	54916-6/$3.95
TEREZA BATISTA: Home from the Wars	34645-1/$2.95
TIETA	50815-X/$4.95
TWO DEATHS OF QUINCAS WATERYELL	50047-7/$2.50
THE VIOLENT LAND	47696-7/$2.75

■By Gabriel García Márquez

THE AUTUMN OF THE PATRIARCH	51300-5/$2.95
IN EVIL HOUR	52167-9/$2.75
ONE HUNDRED YEARS OF SOLITUDE	59097-2/$3.50

AVON Paperbacks

Available wherever paperbacks are sold, or directly from the publisher. Include 50¢ per copy for postage and handling; allow 6-8 weeks for delivery. Avon Books, Mail Order Dept., 224 West 57th St., N.Y., N.Y. 10019.

2 Lat Am 1-83

AVON BARD
DISTINGUISHED
LATIN AMERICAN FICTION